DRAGON SLAYERS' ACADEMY™

The Early Adventures

By Kate McMullan
Cover illustration by Stephen Gilpin
Illustrated by Bill Basso

Grosset & Dunlap
An Imprint of Penguin Random House

In memory of Bill Basso

GROSSET & DUNLAP
Penguin Young Readers Group
An Imprint of Penguin Random House LLC

Penguin supports copyright. Copyright fuels creativity, encourages diverse voices, promotes free speech, and creates a vibrant culture. Thank you for buying an authorized edition of this book and for complying with copyright laws by not reproducing, scanning, or distributing any part of it in any form without permission. You are supporting writers and allowing Penguin to continue to publish books for every reader.

The publisher does not have any control over and does not assume any responsibility for author or third-party websites or their content.

The Library of Congress has cataloged the individual books under the following Control Numbers: *The New Kid at School*: 97015520, *Revenge of the Dragon Lady*: 97031171, *Class Trip to the Cave of Doom*: 98035524, *A Wedding for Wiglaf?*: 98041532.

ISBN 9781524790653   10 9 8 7 6 5 4 3 2 1

Table of Contents

DRAGON SLAYERS' ACADEMY 1

THE NEW KID AT SCHOOL

KATE McMULLAN

Chapter 1

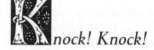nock! Knock!

"Who's there?" Fergus bellowed from inside the hovel.

"A poor minstrel!" came a voice from out in the blizzard.

"A poor minstrel who?" Fergus called.

"Please! I am freezing!" cried the minstrel. "This is no time for a joke!"

"Pity!" Fergus yelled. "There's nothing I like better than a good knock-knock!"

He yanked open the door. There stood a snow-covered man with a lute and a pack slung over his shoulder. Icicles hung from his nose and ears. His lips were blue from the cold.

"Be gone, varlet!" Fergus shouted through his dirty yellow beard. "There is no room here!"

Fergus spoke the truth. His whole hovel was but one cramped room, which he shared with his wife, Molwena, and their thirteen sons.

Twelve of these sons were big, beefy lads with greasy yellow hair like their father's. They scowled out the door at the minstrel, shouting, "Be gone! Be gone!"

But the third-eldest son, Wiglaf, was different from his brothers. He was small for his age. He had hair the color of carrots. And he could not bear to see any creature suffer.

When Fergus reached out to slam the door in the shivering minstrel's face, Wiglaf grabbed his arm.

"Wait, Father!" he said. "Could not the minstrel sleep in the pigsty?"

"I sing songs and tell fortunes," the minstrel offered.

"Songs? Fortunes?" Fergus growled. "Pig droppings!"

"I also chop wood, shovel snow, slop pigs, rake dung, scrub floors, and wash dishes," the minstrel added quickly.

"Oh, but we have Wiglaf to do all that," Molwena told him.

"Please!" the minstrel begged through his chattering teeth. "There must be *something* I can do in return for a roof over my head."

Fergus scratched his beard and tried to think.

"He might kill rats for us, Fergus," Molwena suggested. "Wiglaf won't do that."

"Wiglaf feels sorry for the rats," one of the younger brothers told the minstrel.

"Wiglaf won't squish a cockroach," another

brother tattled. "He won't even swat a fly."

"Wiggie never wants to kill anything," complained a third. "I was pulling the legs off a spider once, and—"

"I have it!" Fergus bellowed suddenly. "The minstrel can kill rats to earn his keep!" He grinned. "Show him to the sty, Wiglaf!"

So Wiglaf did just that. And later on he took a bowl of Molwena's cabbage soup out to the minstrel for his supper.

"Ah! Hot soup to warm my cold bones!" The minstrel took a sip. "Gaaach!" he cried, and spat it out.

"It is foul-tasting at first," Wiglaf admitted. "But you'll get used to it."

"I must or I shall starve," the minstrel said. "Talk to me, lad, while I try to get it down." Then he held his nose and jammed a spoonful into his mouth.

"You are lucky to bed out here with the pigs," Wiglaf told him. "The sty smells far better than our hovel, for my father believes that bathing causes madness. And Daisy, here"—he patted the head of a plump young pig sitting next to him—"she is my best friend. And far better company than my brothers. They only like to fight and bloody each other's noses."

Wiglaf rubbed his own nose. It was still tender from one of his brother's fists.

"They gang up on me something awful," he added. "Then they call me a blister and a runt because I will not fight back. I know it is foolish," he went on, "but sometimes I dream that one day I will become a mighty hero. Would not *that* surprise my brothers!"

"No doubt it would," the minstrel said. He jammed one last spoonful of soup into his mouth. Then he burped. "Ah! That's better. Now, my boy, I know some tales of mighty heroes. Would you care to hear one?"

"I would, indeed!" Wiglaf exclaimed.

No one had ever told Wiglaf a tale before. Oh, Molwena sometimes told him what she would do to him if he did not wash the dishes. And Fergus often told him how he was no use at all in the cabbage fields. But those tales were not so much fun to hear.

Wiglaf settled down in the straw next to his pig to listen. The tale was indeed about a mighty hero. A hero who tried to slay a dragon named Gorzil.

When at last the minstrel came to the end, his voice dropped low. "Then Gorzil roared a roar of thunder. Bolts of lightning shot from his nose. And from out of the fire and smoke came a CRUNCH...CRUNCH...CRUNCH! And a mighty GULP!

"When the smoke cleared, the knight and his steed were gone," the minstrel said. "But Gorzil was sitting high on his pile of gold—using the knight's own sword for a toothpick."

"No!" cried Wiglaf.

"'Tis true," the minstrel told the boy. "My grandfather was a dragon hunter. He saw it happen with his own two eyes—well, with his one good eye, anyway."

"Pray, tell," Wiglaf asked, "who finally killed this dragon?"

"Oh, Gorzil is still very much alive." The minstrel grew thoughtful. "My grandfather told me that every dragon has a secret weakness. Take Old Snart, for instance. For years, that dragon set fire to villages for sport. Then one day Sir Gilford stuck out his tongue and said, 'Nonny-nonny poo-poo, you old sissy!' Well, Old Snart hated to be teased. He began whimpering and crying until he collapsed in a pool of tears. He hardly noticed when Sir Gilford sliced off his head."

"And what is the dragon Gorzil's weakness?" Wiglaf asked.

"That," said the minstrel, "no one knows." He picked up his lute. "I have written a song about Gorzil. Listen:

"Gorzil is a dragon, a greedy one is he,
From his jaws of terror, villagers do flee.
Gorzil burps up clouds of smoke,
Shoots lightning from his snout....
Where, oh, where's the hero
Who'll find his secret out?"

From that night on, Wiglaf brought the minstrel a bowl of cabbage soup for supper. In return, the minstrel told Wiglaf many a dragon tale. And he taught the boy many a useful skill: how to stand on his head; how to wiggle his ears; and how to imitate the call of a lovesick toad.

By the time the snow began to melt, he had even taught the boy how to read and write.

Then one spring morning, Wiglaf brought the pigs their slop and found the minstrel packing.

"Are you off for good?" Wiglaf asked sadly.

"Aye, lad. A minstrel must wander," the minstrel explained. "And"—he burped—"eat something besides cabbage soup. But here, give me your hand. Before I go, I shall tell your fortune."

Wiglaf held out his palm. The minstrel studied it for a long time.

"What do you see?" Wiglaf finally asked.

"Something I never thought to see," the minstrel replied. "The lines on your palm say that you were born to be a mighty hero!"

"Me?" Wiglaf cried. "Are you sure?"

The minstrel nodded. "In all my years of telling fortunes, I have never been wrong."

"Imagine!" Wiglaf exclaimed. "But what brave deed will I do?"

"That," said the minstrel, "you must discover for yourself. Now I must be off. I shall miss you, Wiglaf."

"Wait!" Wiglaf said. He reached into his tunic and pulled out a tattered piece of cloth. "This is all I have left of...well, of something I had when I was very young. I carry it with me always, for good luck." He held the rag out to the minstrel. "Here. I should like you to have it."

"Keep your good-luck charm, Wiglaf," the minstrel said, shouldering his lute. "The road a hero travels is never an easy one. I fear you shall need much luck."

And with that he was gone.

Chapter 2

"Knock! Knock!" Fergus bellowed one fine summer morning at the breakfast table.

Wiglaf didn't answer. He poked at his cabbage pancake, lost in his own thoughts.

It had been months since the minstrel went away. And as far as Wiglaf could tell, he had not become a hero. True, he had saved a chipmunk from drowning in the pigs' water trough. And he had rescued six spiders from his brothers' cruel hands. But surely these were not the deeds of a mighty hero.

Wiglaf kept brooding. He never noticed Fergus bending down close to his ear.

"KNOCK! KNOCK!" Fergus shouted.

Wiglaf jumped. "Who—who's there?"

"Harry!" Fergus cried.

"Harry who?" asked Wiglaf.

"Harry up and eat your pancakes!" Fergus roared. "We go to the Pinwick Fair today!"

"Hooray!" yelled one of Wiglaf's little brothers. "Jugglers and lepers! Let us be off!"

"And so we shall be," Molwena promised, "as soon as Wiglaf does the dishes."

"We could be off sooner if someone dried," Wiglaf hinted.

"Nah," said the eldest brother. "We'll wait."

And so Wiglaf scrubbed the dishes. Then he dried them. Then he put them away.

At last the family set off for the village.

Just outside Pinwick, Fergus stopped beside the village message tree. He squinted at a new notice tacked to its trunk.

"Wiglaf!" Fergus shouted. "The minstrel showed you how to make sense of these squiggles. Tell us what this sign says!"

Wiglaf stepped up and read: "Dragon Slayers' Academy."

Fergus frowned. "Acada...*what?*"

"Academy," Wiglaf repeated. "It means school."

"I know *that*," his father said. "Go on."

"We teach our students to slay dragons," Wiglaf read.

Slay dragons? Wiglaf thought with growing interest. *Heroes slayed dragons!*

"And," he read on, "they bring the dragons' hoards home to *you!*"

"The dragons' hoards?" Fergus scratched his armpit thoughtfully. "That would be... what?"

"Gold and jewels, most likely," Wiglaf replied.

"Blazing King Ken's britches!" Fergus roared. "Read it all!" Which is just what Wiglaf was dying to do:

Is there a lazy lad hanging about your hovel? Is he eating more than his share of your good cabbage soup? Don't you wish he could earn his keep?

"I'll say," snorted Molwena.

Dragon Slayers' Academy is your answer! Feast your eyes on just a few of our classes:

- *How to Stalk a Fire-Breather*
- *How to Get Close to a Dragon*
- *How to Get Even Closer*
- *How to Get Really, Really Close*
- *101 Ways to Slay*

Best of all, we will teach your boy how to bring a dragon's golden hoard home to you!

*Just look at what some of our fine
lads have done:*

Baldrick the Bold

*Baldrick slew three dragons! With
their golden hoards, he bought his lucky
parents a 450-room castle!*

"That would do for us," Molwena
muttered.

Torblad the Terrible

*Two kills. Two hoards. Now his mum
and pop just lie about and watch other
folk work.*

"Oh, boy!" said Fergus.

Angus the Avenger

*Angus slew a whole nest of dragon
young! His parents now dress in nothing but silk and velvet.*

"Do they, now?!" Molwena exclaimed. "I wonder how much this school costs."

The fee? Only 7 pennies! (Plus a teensy part of each hoard.) Send us your sons! We turn useless lads into HEROES who go for the gold!

Signed,
Mordred the Marvelous, Headmaster, DSA (Located just off Huntsman's Path, east of the Dark Forest)

Dragon slaying, thought Wiglaf. It sounded pretty gruesome. But dragons were evil. They deserved to be slain—didn't they? And who slew them? Mighty heroes, that's who!

Maps tacked to the tree showed the way from Pinwick to Dragon Slayers' Academy. Wiglaf pulled one off and stared at it. Here was a path he might follow to become a hero!

"Father?" Wiglaf began eagerly, "I would—"

"Quiet!" Fergus barked. He turned to his eldest son. "Do you want to go to the acad... to the school?" he asked him.

The eldest picked at a scab on his ear. "Would I get in trouble for fighting and knocking other boys' teeth out?" he asked.

Fergus nodded. "You might."

"I wouldn't like that," the eldest declared.

Wiglaf tried again. "Father, I—"

"Shush!" Fergus turned to his second-eldest. "Do you want to go to the school?" he asked him.

The second-eldest scratched a bedbug bite on his neck. "Would I have to comb my hair and change my britches?" he asked.

Fergus nodded again. "Most likely."

"Then I won't go," the second-eldest said.

"I will, Father!" Wiglaf exclaimed. "Pray, send me!"

But Fergus only rolled his eyes and turned to his fourth-eldest. "You're a big, strapping lad," he began. "How would you—"

"Wait, Father!" Wiglaf cut in. "Think on this: If I slay a dragon, I shall bring you a mountain of gold! You would like that, would you not?"

"Yes...." Fergus nodded slowly.

"And if the dragon gets the better of me?" Wiglaf went on. "Well, you say I am no use to you in the cabbage fields anyway."

"Hmm...." Fergus tugged at a chicken bone that had been tangled in his beard all week. "I have it!" he roared at last. "I shall send *Wiglaf* to the dragon school! He is no use to me in the cabbage fields anyway!"

"That's a fine idea, Fergus," Molwena put in. "But what about the seven pennies? Where would we get that kind of money?"

Fergus shrugged. "That pig of his should bring seven pennies."

"You mean, sell Daisy?" Wiglaf cried.

Wiglaf's younger brother wiped his nose on

his sleeve. "Daddy?" he said. "When Wiglaf goes, can I have his goatskin to sleep under?"

"Yes, all right," replied their father.

"But—" Wiglaf began.

"Can I have his spoon, then?" asked his even younger brother.

"Yes, yes," answered Fergus.

"Can I have his boots?" asked his still younger brother. "And his britches and his tunic?"

"Wait!" Wiglaf cried. "I'm not dead, am I? I still need my clothes! And I shall never sell Daisy! Never!"

"Oh, do be quiet," Molwena scolded. "How else are you going to get seven pennies?"

Wiglaf folded his arms across his chest. "I shall find a way."

"Mommy," one of the younger brothers whined, "I want to go to the fair! I want to see the two-headed calf."

"Of course you do!" Molwena exclaimed.

"And we don't want to miss the hanging." She turned away from the tree, and the rest of the family followed.

All but Wiglaf. He straggled behind, thinking. He was going away to Dragon Slayers' Academy! And, somehow, he was going to keep Daisy by his side.

Wiglaf smiled. At last he was on his way to becoming a mighty hero.

Chapter 3

"Well, farewell!" Wiglaf said the next morning at dawn. Fergus and Molwena and a few of his brothers had gotten up to see him off.

Fergus slapped Wiglaf on the back and roared, "Knock! Knock!"

"Who's there?" called a little brother.

"Oliver!" said Fergus.

"Oliver who?" asked another little brother.

"Oliver troubles will be over when Wiglaf comes home with the gold!" Fergus cried. He slapped him on the back again.

"Off you go," Molwena said. "Get a good price for the pig."

"And don't come home without the gold!" Fergus added.

Wiglaf picked up his pack. Inside were six cabbage dumplings, a loaf of cabbage bread, and a pickled cabbage tart. He had also put in a length of rope, the map, and his lucky rag.

"Ready, Daisy?" Wiglaf asked.

The faithful pig glanced up at him and wagged her curly tail. Then the two of them set off for Dragon Slayers' Academy.

They walked south all morning. Around noon, they came to Nowhere Swamp. The minstrel had told Wiglaf tales of this spot. Hungry serpents lurked in the slimy water. Hungry vultures circled overhead. Mad hermits lived in every cave and hollow tree. And most of them were hungry, too.

But worst of all was the quicksand. It was so quick it could suck a boy down—*slurp!*—before he could cry for help. A traveler had to be very careful to get across it with his life.

Wiglaf studied his map closely. "We must cross here, Daisy," he said. "I shall carry you."

Wiglaf picked up the pig and started along the spine of rocks jutting out from the quicksand. Wiglaf knew that one false step and—*slurp!*—he would never be a hero.

On a big, flat rock halfway across, Wiglaf stopped. He put Daisy down and searched the swamp to see how far they still had to go.

"Daisy!" Wiglaf cried. "A pointed hat is sinking in the quicksand! And look! There is a *head* beneath the hat!"

Daisy squealed in alarm.

Wiglaf cupped his hands to his mouth. "Stay where you are!" he shouted to the head. "I shall save you!"

Wiglaf grabbed the rope from his pack. His heart thumped. He never thought that he would be a hero *this* soon! But before he could throw the rope, the hat and head started to rise.

Wiglaf watched, amazed, as a man with a long white beard floated up, out of the sand. He wore a wide-sleeved blue robe dotted with silver stars. He glided over the quicksand toward Wiglaf and Daisy.

Now Daisy squealed in fright.

The man came to a stop in front of Wiglaf. "Don't you have anything better to do than annoy me?" he grumbled. "And turn off that pig!"

Instantly, Daisy stopped squealing.

"I am sorry," Wiglaf managed. "Are—are you a wizard?"

"No, I'm a fairy princess!" the man snapped. "Of course I'm a wizard. You know anyone else who wears a long blue robe with stars on it? I don't think so. Zelnoc's the name," he went on. "And your name is...wait." The wizard squeezed his eyes shut. "Don't tell me. It's coming. Ah! I have it. Wigwam! No...Waglump!"

"Close," Wiglaf said. "I am Wiglaf. And this is my pig, Daisy."

"Charmed." The wizard gave a little wave. "Now, Wuglop, what was all that yelling about? And what's with the rope?"

"I was going to rescue you from the quicksand," Wiglaf explained.

Zelnoc shook his head. "Do you know nothing of wizards, my boy? I wasn't sinking. I was in for repairs. This part of the swamp is known as Wizards' Bog. The quicksand here has strong powers. You see, sometimes my spells go wrong...." He shrugged. "It's not your problem. So tell me. What are you doing out here in the middle of Nowhere?"

"I am on my way to Dragon Slayers' Academy," Wiglaf said proudly.

"You're kidding!" Zelnoc exclaimed. "*You* are a dragon slayer?"

"Not yet," Wiglaf admitted. "But a minstrel told my fortune. He said that I was born to be a hero. And heroes slay dragons, do they not?"

"Some do, I suppose," the wizard said. "Well, I wish you luck, Wicklamp. And speaking of wishes, what'll it be?"

"I beg your pardon?" Wiglaf said.

"Your wish!" Zelnoc repeated. "You *did* interrupt me, it's true. But you meant well. And Wizard Rule Number 364 says every good deed must be rewarded. So wish away, Wigloop. But make it snappy. I haven't got all day."

"All right," Wiglaf agreed. "I wish for... seven pennies!"

Zelnoc shook his head. "Sorry, kid. Wizards never carry cash."

"I see." Wiglaf thought for a moment. Then he said, "How about a suit of armor?"

"No, no, no," the wizard scolded. "Only *knights* wear armor!"

Wiglaf sighed. "What should I wish for?"

"A sword," Zelnoc told him.

"All right," said Wiglaf. "I wish for a sword."

"An excellent choice!" exclaimed the wizard. "And have I got a sword for you!"

Zelnoc reached up his left sleeve and pulled out a stumpy metal blade. It was badly bent, dented, and covered with rust.

"This is Surekill," Zelnoc said. "It was made for dragon slaying. It has great power."

"Oh, is it a magic sword?" Wiglaf asked hopefully.

"Would I give you any other kind?" Zelnoc rolled his eyes. "Now, here's what you do. Point Surekill at your enemy and say..." The wizard frowned. "What is it, now? 'Surekill, go get 'em!'? No... 'Surekill, do your thing!'? No. But it's something like that. Anyway, when you do get it right, Surekill will leap from your hand and obey."

"Uh...thank you," Wiglaf said, taking the weapon and tucking it into his belt. He supposed a rusty, dented sword was better than no sword at all.

Zelnoc glanced at Daisy. "What about the pig?" he asked. "Does she have a wish?"

"If only she could talk, she might tell you," Wiglaf answered.

"Talk?" Zelnoc's eyes lit up. "I have just the thing! My speech spell!"

The wizard pushed up his sleeves, stretched his hands toward Daisy, and began to chant: "Oink-a-la, doink-a-la, fee fi fig! This pig shall be a talking pig!"

Daisy blinked, and very softly she said, "Iglaf-Way?"

"She speaks!" Wiglaf cried. "Yet in what strange tongue?"

"Maybe Greek?" the wizard guessed.

"E-may, alking-tay!" Daisy burbled happily.

"I know!" Wiglaf exclaimed. "'Tis Pig Latin!"

"Excuse me?" Zelnoc said.

"Pig Latin," Wiglaf said. "You know—where you take the first sound in a word and put it at the end. Then you add the 'ay' sound. Pig becomes 'ig-pay.' Do you see?"

"Pig Latin, my foot!" Zelnoc moaned. "My spell went wrong!"

"O-nay idding-kay!" Daisy scoffed.

"Stop, pig!" Zelnoc cried. "That crazy language makes my beard twitch." He shuddered. "I'm in worse shape than I thought. And the Wizards' Convention is only two weeks away."

Zelnoc turned and began gliding back to the center of the bog.

"Good-bye, Waglap!" he called. "Good luck with the dragons!"

"Good-bye!" Wiglaf called back.

"O-say ong-lay!" Daisy squealed.

Then, with a loud *slurp*, the quicksand swallowed up the wizard, this time hat and all.

Chapter 4

Wiglaf checked his map by the light of the full moon. Yes, this had to be the place—Dragon Slayers' Academy.

"In truth, this is not what I expected," Wiglaf muttered.

"Uck-yay," Daisy agreed.

Wiglaf and Daisy stood at the edge of a moat filled with greenish, foul-smelling water. It reminded Wiglaf, in many ways, of Molwena's cabbage soup.

A rickety drawbridge led over the water to a gatehouse set in the middle of the broken-down castle wall. A tattered blue banner waved above the door. Bold letters on it spelled out DSA.

Wiglaf drew a deep breath and started across the drawbridge. Daisy trotted at his side.

Wiglaf pulled a chain by the gatehouse door. A bell sounded from deep within.

After a time, the door cracked open. A short man with big eyes stared out at the travelers. He held a torch in one hand.

"Yes?" he said.

"I am Wiglaf, sir," Wiglaf offered. "I am here to study."

"Welcome to DSA!" the man said, opening the door. Wiglaf saw that he wore an apron. "Odd time to arrive, midnight," the man went on. "And school started two weeks ago. But no matter. First things first." He held out his hand. "Seven pennies, please."

"Alas," Wiglaf sighed. "I have no pennies."

The door began to close.

"Wait, sir!" he called. "I—I have half a cabbage dumpling!"

The door banged shut.

"I am a willing worker!" Wiglaf added. "I wash dishes and—"

The door opened a few inches. The man stuck his head out.

"You are skilled at washing dishes?" he asked.

Wiglaf nodded. "Very skilled."

"Well, that suits me better than seven pennies any day." The man opened wide the door. "Come in, come in. I am Frypot, school cook. And former dishwasher."

"Oh, I thank you, kind sir!" Wiglaf exclaimed.

"But say not a word of this to Headmaster Mordred," Frypot warned. "He will put the thumbscrews to me if he finds out."

"Not a word, sir," Wiglaf promised. Then he and Daisy started through the door.

"Hold up now!" Frypot cried. "No pigs allowed!"

"But, sir," Wiglaf began. "This is no ordinary pig! Just listen. Daisy, say hello to the kind man."

"Ello-hay, Ypot-Fray!" Daisy said.

"Zounds!" Frypot exclaimed. "A pig that speaks Pig Latin!"

Frypot knelt down next to Daisy.

"Ello-hay, iggy-pay," he said slowly and loudly. "Oh, I shall make you a comfy pallet in the henhouse! Yes, just as soon as I sign in our new dishwasher—er, I mean student."

Then Frypot lit the way through the gatehouse, across the castle yard, and up a stone stairway into the crumbling castle.

Just inside the door, Frypot stuck his torch into a holder on the wall. Then he sat down at a desk and opened a thick book.

"Full name?" he asked.

"Wiglaf of Pinwick."

"Age?"

"This shall be my twelfth summer."

"Skills?"

"Washing dishes," began Wiglaf, "slopping pigs, raking dung—"

"I meant any skills that might be useful in dragon slaying," Frypot said.

Wiglaf thought for a moment. "Nothing comes to mind," he answered.

"Class I, then." Frypot shut the book. He opened a cupboard and took out a blue tunic and a helmet. White letters on the tunic spelled out DSA. He gave them to Wiglaf. "Your uniform," he said.

"The kitchen's that way," Frypot added, handing Wiglaf the torch. "You can start on the dishes while I settle your pig."

Then the cook led Daisy toward the door. "Ome-cay, iggy-pay," he said, "and tell me how you came by your enchantment. I never cook bacon, you know. Well, hardly ever...."

"What a poor sword!" Wiglaf heard someone exclaim.

He half-opened one eye. He had not had much sleep. Frypot had not told him how very, *very* many dirty dishes there would be.

Now Wiglaf saw two boys in DSA tunics standing at the foot of his cot. One was sandy-haired and plump. The other had straight brown hair and a serious face. He was holding Surekill.

"Have you ever drawn this sword in battle?" the boy asked.

"No," Wiglaf answered.

"Have you sliced off anyone's head with it?"

"Of course not!" Wiglaf exclaimed.

"And I'll wager you have never killed a dragon with it, either."

"No," Wiglaf admitted. "But the sword is called Surekill," he added. "So perhaps I shall. I am called Wiglaf."

"I am Eric." The boy tossed Surekill back onto Wiglaf's cot. "I sleep there." He pointed to the far side of the room.

Wiglaf turned to see one of many lumpy cots just like his own. On the wall above it hung a certificate which read: SIR LANCELOT FAN CLUB. Next to that hung a tapestry. It showed a knight plunging a sword into a dragon. Blood gushed from the dragon's side. *Yuck!* thought Wiglaf.

"I have not yet killed a dragon," Eric was saying. "But soon I shall. Not for the gold, but to rid the world of evil! I want—"

"Pray, save it, Eric," the plump boy cut in.

"Or we shall miss breakfast." He turned to Wiglaf, adding, "Don't worry. We are not all so eager as Eric."

Wiglaf put on his DSA tunic and helmet, and followed his roommates to a huge dining hall.

Boys of all sizes sat at long wooden tables labeled "Class I," "Class II," and "Class III." A big boy was tossing slices of burnt toast through the air. Other boys punched and poked and pinched each other for the honor of catching them.

The sight made Wiglaf feel a little homesick.

Wiglaf got in line and picked up his tray.

"What's for breakfast?" he asked Eric.

"Fried eel on toast," Eric replied as he took a heaping plateful.

"*Eel?*" Wiglaf cried.

Eric nodded. "Mordred says eating eel is

part of our training," he explained. "Dragon hunters must learn to live on what can be found near a dragon's lair."

The boys carried their trays to the Class I table. Then Wiglaf watched as Eric scooped up a spoonful of greasy eel and eagerly stuffed it into his mouth.

"Ugh!" Wiglaf groaned. "How do dragon hunters do it?"

The plump boy leaned over toward him. "They don't," he whispered. "Eels live in the castle moat, so they do not cost Mordred a cent. *That* is the real reason we are served eel so often."

"How often?" Wiglaf asked in dismay.

"Too often," the boy replied. "By the way, I am Angus."

Wiglaf stared in awe. "Angus the Avenger?"

"Oh, you saw the notice." Angus smiled shyly. "Mordred only made me sound fierce to attract fierce pupils to his school."

"Then...you never killed a nest of dragon young?" Wiglaf asked.

"Not exactly," Angus admitted. "I stumbled over an old dragon nest in the forest once and squashed some rotten eggs. Whew! Did they ever stink!" He waved a hand in front of his nose. "It took weeks to get the slimy goo off my boots."

"Then Torblad the Terrible and Baldrick the Bold...?" Wiglaf began.

Angus shook his head. "I am afraid my Uncle Mordred sometimes stretches the truth."

"The headmaster is your uncle?" Wiglaf exclaimed. "Imagine! So has anybody here ever killed a dragon?"

"Not yet," Eric piped up. "But soon someone shall—and that someone shall be me!"

Clang! Clang! A bell sounded and Eric slurped up the tail of his eel.

"Finish up," Angus advised Wiglaf.

"Stalking a Fire-Breather Class begins in five minutes. And it is way over in the East Tower."

Wiglaf stared at his fried eel on toast—now cold and gray. Then he left it on his plate and hurried after Angus and Eric.

Chapter 5

iglaf, Eric, and Angus rushed along the castle hallways until they came to a spiraling stone staircase. They ran up the steps, two at a time. When they reached the top of the East Tower, they were panting for breath.

Several boys stood at a window, pulling on a rope. Angus and Eric joined them.

Wiglaf, too, began to pull. "What are we raising?" he asked. "It is quite heavy."

"'Tis Sir Mort," Angus replied. "Our teacher. He has a hard time walking up stairs."

In a moment, Wiglaf saw why. A helmeted head appeared at the window. The boys reached out to pull their teacher in. And Sir Mort crashed to the classroom floor—wearing a full suit of armor.

The boys helped him to his feet.

"Stalking a fire-breather is no easy matter, lads," the old knight began lecturing as he lurched and clattered to the front of the room. "Dragons can hear you coming from miles away. Especially if you have on armor. Clanks something awful."

"Sir?" Eric called. "What about a dragon's sense of smell?"

"Oh, they smell all right." Sir Mort nodded thoughtfully. "Like old cheese, most of them. But I slew a dragon once that smelled exactly like my red wool socks when I wear 'em too long and the mold sets in."

Eric tried again. "I meant, can a dragon smell a dragon hunter?"

"Ah! Good question!" Sir Mort exclaimed. "That's how you learn, lads! By asking questions!" He looked around the room. "Are there any more questions?"

A tall, scared-looking boy raised his hand. "How close dare we stalk a dragon without danger?" he asked in a shaky voice.

"*That*," Angus whispered to Wiglaf, "is Torblad the Terrible."

"How close!" Sir Mort exclaimed. "An excellent question. Excellent! You will go far, lad! Next question?"

Eric's hand shot up again. *He certainly is eager,* Wiglaf thought.

"Yesterday you said we must stalk different dragons in different ways," Eric said. "Can you give us an example?"

"Certainly I can." Sir Mort nodded, smiling. "Easy as pie."

Eric and the rest of the class waited. But Sir Mort only kept nodding and smiling.

"Sir?" Eric said at last. "Will you *show* us what you mean?"

"Good idea!" The old knight jangled to the center of the room.

"Take cave-dwelling dragons. They have excellent hearing," Sir Mort explained. "So they must be approached on the sly. I use what I call the Slide 'n' Glide. I stand sideways to the cave like this." Sir Mort turned sideways to the class. "And I slide my right foot out, like this." Sir Mort slid his right foot out.

Unfortunately, the old stone floors of the castle were far smoother than the ground outside a dragon's cave. Sir Mort's boot kept sliding and sliding...and sliding. Until the old knight clanked to the floor in a perfect split. His visor slammed down over his face.

"Hoist me up, lads!" Sir Mort cried in a muffled voice.

Eric and two other boys gripped their teacher under the arms and pulled him up.

"Ah, that's better." Sir Mort pushed his

visor back up. "Slippery devils, these boots. Reminds me of the time I stalked the dragon Fiffnir. Have I shown you the wound Fiffnir gave me? Nasty wound it is, too."

Sir Mort bent down. He began struggling to pull off the left boot of his armor.

In the distance a bell rang.

Angus spoke up. "Sir Mort, class is over."

"Devilish tight, this boot," Sir Mort grumbled.

"Sir, we must go to Slaying Class now," Angus continued. "Coach Plungett gets vexed if we are late."

"Go then, lads. Go!" Sir Mort said. "My wound will wait. Got it the year of the grasshopper plague. No, the year before. Couldn't have walked to Constantinople. Not with this wound. No, it must have been..."

Quietly, Wiglaf followed Angus and Eric and the other future dragon slayers down the spiral staircase. He was amazed at how much he had learned of dragon stalking in one short morning!

"Step it up, lads!" Coach Plungett called as Class I ran out into the castle yard. The large man's long brown pageboy-style hair blew gently in the breeze. "Ten laps around the castle," he ordered. "Can't kill a dragon if you're not in shape!"

By lap three, Eric was way ahead of the others. Wiglaf was way behind. He began to worry that slopping pigs and washing dishes had not prepared him well for dragon slaying.

But after the laps, the coach ordered the boys to take a deep breath and hold it for the count of fifty.

"If a dragon spews out poison," he told them, "the longer you can hold your breath, the better. Ready? And! One...two...three...."

Wiglaf smiled as he held his breath. Living

in the smelly hovel with his unwashed family had given him plenty of practice at this skill! He alone made it to the count of fifty.

"Good work!" Coach Plungett told him. "Now before we start slaying, why don't you give the DSA cheer for our new boy? Belt it out now, boys!"

At once, the whole class began shouting at the top of their lungs:

> *"Rooty-toot-ho! Rooty-toot-hey!*
> *We are the boys from DSA!*
> *We slay dragons, yes we do!*
> *Big ones! Bony ones! Fat ones, too!*
> *We slay dragons, young and old!*
> *We slay dragons, grab their gold!*
> *Yea! Yea! For good old DSA—Hey!"*

"Hey!" Coach clapped at the end of the cheer. "All right now, line up in front of Old Blodgett. Quickly, lads. Go on!"

Wiglaf and the others lined up in front of a

large dragon. It wasn't a real dragon, of course. Old Blodgett was only a wooden one covered with cloth and stuffed with straw.

"Slaying is the most important class here at DSA," Coach told the boys. "You can find a dragon. You can stalk a dragon. But if you cannot *slay* a dragon, you cannot get a hoard.

"Today we shall practice Slaying Method Number Seven, the Throat Thrust. Aim here." Coach Plungett pointed the tip of his sword just under Old Blodgett's chin where a target had been painted. "Not many scales in that spot. Watch me now!"

Coach Plungett faced the false dragon. He drew his weapon, galloped a few steps, and with a toss of his brown pageboy, thrust his sword deep into the dragon's neck.

Wiglaf cringed. He knew that no blood would spill from this dragon. Still his stomach did flip-flops.

Wiglaf watched with growing dread as each

boy took a turn stabbing the practice dragon. When his turn came, he drew Surekill, galloped toward the dragon, and stopped.

"Go on, boy!" Coach Plungett urged him.

Wiglaf backed up. He gripped Surekill more tightly. He stared at the target on the dragon's throat. He galloped forward again ...and stopped.

"Blazing King Ken's britches!" Coach cried. "Aim here!" He pointed at the target.

Wiglaf backed up once more. He swallowed. If he could not plunge his sword into this dummy dragon, what hope did he have of ever slaying a *real* one? Wiglaf took a step toward Old Blodgett. Then another. And another.

"I cannot watch!" Coach Plungett moaned. He turned away in disgust.

But Wiglaf kept on. Faster and faster he came. At the last minute, he closed his eyes.

"Haiii-yah!" He thrust Surekill up toward the dragon's chin.

But somehow Wiglaf missed. He went flying past the practice dragon and landed on a bale of straw. His eyes popped open. Around him, boys were hooting and pointing.

Wiglaf glanced at Surckill. His heart nearly stopped. He had missed the practice dragon. But he had speared some small, brown, furry creature! There it was, stuck on the end of his sword!

Why is everyone laughing, Wiglaf wondered, *when I have so cruelly killed a ...uh...?*

"I'll take that!" growled the coach.

Wiglaf looked up to see a very bald Coach Plungett snatch the hairy thing from the end of Surekill and angrily set it on his head.

Only then did Wiglaf understand what creature he had murdered. Coach Plungett's own brown pageboy wig!

Chapter 6

Wiglaf picked at his lunch of boiled eel on a bun. Coach Plungett was sure to give him an F in slaying now. He had messed up royally—and on his very first day of school.

"Come on, Wiglaf. Eat up!" Angus told him. "You do *not* want to be late for Mordred's class."

Mordred! Wiglaf shuddered. *What would the headmaster do to a new boy who had nearly slayed the slaying coach?*

With dark thoughts, Wiglaf followed Angus to a stone-walled classroom. As the boys sat down on a rickety bench, a huge man in a red cloak strode through the door. Thick black hair sprouted from his head. His violet eyes bulged like overripe plums.

"Atten-*tion!*" Mordred the Marvelous called.

The students leaped to their feet. Wiglaf did, too.

"At ease!" Mordred commanded.

The boys sat down.

"Let us review," the headmaster said. "Why are you here at Dragon Slayers' Academy?"

"To learn to slay evil dragons!" Eric called out at once. "To make the world safe for little children! To save villagers from—"

"Yes, yes," Mordred interrupted, holding up a hand heavy with gold rings. "That is all well and good. But what about yesterday's lesson? What did I say? Anyone? Baldrick?"

A small freckle-faced boy with a runny nose stood up. "We are here to learn how to get a dragon's golden hoard, sir! And bring it back to you, sir!"

"Correct!" Mordred grinned, showing a shiny gold front tooth. "To bring me gold! And"—he coughed—"to take some...a teeny bit...maybe...home to your"—he coughed again—"parents."

He cleared his throat. "Now, who remembers how to find a cave-dwelling dragon?"

Again, Eric was the first to answer. "Look for burned spots on shrubs and bushes!" he called. "And big footprints with three long toes!"

Mordred nodded. "And when you spot the dragon...what must you look out for?"

"Beware flames of death!" Eric shouted. "Beware a dragon's poison spit!"

"Correct, Eric." Mordred sighed and looked around. "Anyone *else?*"

"Beware the eyes that never close!" Eric called again. "Beware the knife-sharp teeth! Beware the powerful, lashing tail!"

"Thank you, *Eric,*" Mordred said. "Now,

what else must a dragon hunter know in order to *slay* such a beast?"

"How to talk to a dragon!" Eric called. "How to be brave!"

Mordred nodded. "Anything else?"

At last Eric was quiet. And so were all the other boys.

But Wiglaf had listened well to the minstrel's dragon tales. He knew there was one thing that Eric had not mentioned. Timidly, he raised his hand.

Mordred's bulging eyes lit on him. "Ah, the new boy! The one who scalped Coach Plungett!" The headmaster chuckled. "So, new boy, what else should a dragon hunter know?"

"A dragon's secret weakness?" Wiglaf said meekly.

"That's right!" Mordred's eyebrows shot up.

"Oh, everybody knows *that*," Eric complained.

"Let the new boy tell what he knows of dragon secrets, Eric," Mordred said. "Maybe you will learn something."

"From *him?*" Eric muttered. "Not likely."

"Well, new boy?" Mordred said. "Pray, tell us what you know!"

"I—I know very little...." Wiglaf began.

"See?" Eric cut in. "What did I tell you?"

But the headmaster ignored him. "New boy," he said, "know you the secret weakness of the dragon Gorzil?"

"No, sir," Wiglaf answered. "His weakness is still a secret."

"Too true." Mordred sighed sadly. "But it would be useful to know it. For Gorzil is rumored to be in the Dark Forest. My scout Yorick is there now. As soon as he finds Gorzil's cave, I shall send my best boys out to slay him. Slay him, and claim his great big golden hoard!"

These words were barely out of Mordred's

mouth when a small man burst into the classroom. Branches and leaves were tied to his tunic, as if he were trying to disguise himself as a bush.

"Yorick!" Mordred exclaimed. "Back so soon? What news from the Dark Forest?"

"My lord," Yorick began, "Gorzil has moved to a cave outside the village of Toenail."

"Toenail!" Torblad shrieked. "My family lives in Toenail!"

"Sit down, Torblad," Mordred snarled. "Go on, Yorick."

"My lord," Yorick said, "the Toenailians have brought Gorzil all their gold. Now he swears to burn Toenail to the ground unless a son and a daughter of the village are outside his cave tomorrow. Tomorrow at dawn, in time for breakfast!"

"Oh, that's nice of Gorzil," Torblad said, cheering up. "Having company for breakfast."

"You ninny!" Mordred cried. "They are to *be* his breakfast!" The headmaster turned back to his scout. "So! I shall send boys out to slay Gorzil this very afternoon!"

Then a look of horror crossed his face.

"Egad!" he exclaimed. "Class II and Class III just left on that blasted field trip to see the petrified dragon skeleton! That means I shall have to send Class I boys!"

"Pray, send me!" Eric cried, falling to his knees.

"Yes, yes," Mordred said. "But remember, we have a buddy system here. I'll need another volunteer." He looked around the room. "Anyone but Angus. If I sent you, I'd never hear the end of it from your mother. All right, who will it be?"

No hands went up.

"Come now," Mordred coaxed. "Gorzil is not so bad!"

Still no hands went up.

"My patience grows thin!" Mordred warned. Then his violet eyes lit upon Wiglaf.

"You! New boy!" he boomed. "You seem to know a fair bit about dragons. And I chanced to look at the register book at lunchtime. You never paid your seven pennies!"

"That is so," Wiglaf began. "But—" He stopped. He had promised Frypot to say not a word about their dishwashing deal.

"No buts!" Mordred cried. "You shall go with Eric! And you shall pay your seven pennies out of Gorzil's gold!"

"Aw, sir!" Eric cried. "Pray, pick someone else! Wiglaf has not even been here a whole day! He knows nothing of slaying!"

"*You* slay Gorzil, then!" Mordred shouted. "Let him pull the cart for the dragon's hoard. Now, be off! You must reach Gorzil's cave by dawn. What are you waiting for? Go!"

Chapter 7

"Ready, Wiglaf?" Eric called as he hurried toward the gatehouse.

Wiglaf was bent over, trying to fix a wobbly wheel on the hoard cart. He glanced up and was nearly blinded by the glare from Eric's slaying outfit.

Eric stood proudly before him in a gleaming silver helmet. He carried a broad silver shield. And a wide silver belt held his sword.

Wiglaf had only Surekill.

"What fine gear," Wiglaf told Eric.

"Yes," Eric agreed. "I sent away for it from the Sir Lancelot Fan Club catalog. Come! You shall pull the cart as Mordred said. Let us be off. My sword is itching to slay the dragon!"

Wiglaf began to slide back the great iron bolt on the gatehouse door. But a yell from Eric made him stop.

"Boar!" Eric cried. "Wild boar!"

Wiglaf turned to see Eric with his sword drawn and his shield up.

"Stand back!" Eric shouted. "I shall slay the charging beast!"

"What beast?" Wiglaf asked. Then he spotted something running toward them across the castle yard. It was Daisy!

"Eric, stop!" Wiglaf shouted. "Stop! That is my own pig, Daisy!"

Eric stopped and glumly lowered his sword. He jammed it back into its scabbard and stomped off, grumbling.

Wiglaf ran to Daisy.

"Iglaf-Way!" she squealed. "Ake-tay ee-may ith-way ou-yay!"

"I cannot, Daisy," Wiglaf said sadly. He squatted down beside her and scratched her bristly ears. "It is too dangerous. For I am off to hunt a dragon."

"Orzil-Gay?" Daisy's voice trembled.

Wiglaf nodded. "Who knows? Perhaps I shall return a hero." He tried to smile. "But if I do not"—he gulped—"if I do not return, I am sure Frypot will take good care of you. Now I—I must go. Farewell, best pig in the world!"

"Arewell-fay, Iglaf-Way!" Daisy called after him. "Ood-gay uck-lay!"

Wiglaf waved and hurried back to the gatehouse. Then he picked up the cart handle. "Let us be off," he said to Eric.

Wiglaf and Eric followed the trail down the hill from Dragon Slayers' Academy. Then they headed north on Huntsman's Path.

They walked beside the Swampy River all afternoon. Strange birds cried out from the stunted trees along the way. Hairy-legged spiders dropped down on them from over-hanging branches. Once an angry troll threatened them with his club. But Wiglaf was not afraid. The thought of facing Gorzil was so terrifying that nothing else bothered him.

Well, almost nothing.

"I shall slay Gorzil, no problem!" Eric announced for the two-hundredth time. "I shall plunge my sword into his throat. I shall twist it! Buckets of blood will gush from the dragon's steaming wound! Then I shall—"

"You know," Wiglaf broke in finally, "my sword was made for dragon slaying, too."

"That bent-up old thing?" Eric sneered.

Wiglaf nodded. "A wizard gave it to me," he explained. "When I say magic words, it will leap from my hand and obey."

Eric looked doubtful. "And just what are the magic words?"

"Uh...the wizard had forgotten," Wiglaf mumbled.

"It matters not," Eric scoffed as they came to a fork in Huntsman's Path. One path led to the village of Toenail. The other led into the Dark Forest. "For I shall slay this dragon with my own silvery sword. I shall cut Gorzil to ribbons! I shall—"

Suddenly, Eric stopped talking. He stared at the blackened leaves of a nearby shrub.

"Behold!" he cried. "This bush is scorched!"

Wiglaf bent down to take a closer look. "So it is," he agreed. "Could it be from the hot breath of a dragon?"

"How could it not? And look here!" Eric pointed to the ground. "Footprints!"

Wiglaf stared at a huge three-toed print in the path in front of them. "My, but these footprints are large!" he exclaimed.

"Come!" Eric said. "They will lead us to

Gorzil's cave. Hark!" he added. "What noise is that?"

Wiglaf listened. "It sounds like someone crying."

The sound grew louder. Then a boy and girl about Wiglaf and Eric's age came along on the path from Toenail. Tears streamed down their cheeks.

"What ails you, good travelers?" Eric called to them. "And how can we help?"

"Alackaday!" the boy wailed. "You cannot help us. No one can! My sister Zelda and I are on our way to Gorzil's cave!"

"Do you mean," Wiglaf began, "that you are the son and daughter of the village? That you are to be Gorzil's...breakfast?"

Zelda nodded. "I fear it is so. The Toenail village masters held a lottery. And alas— Gawain and I won!"

"If only a brave knight would slay Gorzil

and save us!" Gawain said. "But there is no hope of that."

Eric yanked his sword from its scabbard and held it high in the air.

"Fear not, young friends," he cried. "Eric the Dragon Slayer is at your service!"

Gawain and Zelda stared at him.

"You?" Zelda said.

Eric nodded.

"You are but a boy!" she scoffed.

Eric sniffed. "I am first in my class at Dragon Slayers' Academy," he replied. "I shall slay Gorzil—no sweat!"

"Do you know how many brave knights have tried and perished in his flames?" Gawain asked.

"Um...no. But—" Eric began.

"Gorzil will toast you like a marshmallow!" Zelda declared. "Unless," she added, "you come up with a clever plan."

"A plan?" Wiglaf said. "What kind of—"

"Change clothes with us," Zelda cut in. "Disguise yourselves as the son and the daughter of Toenail and catch Gorzil off guard!"

At first, Eric looked doubtful. Then he began to smile. "Yes!" he exclaimed. "I can see it now! At dawn, *we* shall appear at the mouth of Gorzil's cave, dressed in your clothing. Gorzil will never suspect that behind my back I have a sword! When the dragon opens his jaws to eat me, I shall whip out my sword and plunge it deep into his throat. His whole body will shudder and—"

"But Eric," Wiglaf broke in. "How can one of *us* pass for a *daughter* of the village?"

But Eric was already taking off his helmet. "Worry not, Wiglaf," he said. "Just be quick and give your tunic to Gawain. Here, Zelda. Take my Sir Lancelot armor." Eric handed the girl his helmet and chain mail. "As soon as we are dressed in their clothes," Eric told Wiglaf, "we shall go thitherward to carry out our plan!"

Chapter 8

The sun dawned on Wiglaf and Eric outside the mouth of Gorzil's cave. With trembling fingers, Wiglaf finished tying his lucky rag to Surekill's hilt. If ever he needed luck, it was now!

Wiglaf adjusted Gawain's baggy tunic and trousers. Then he glanced over at Eric, who was wearing Zelda's sky-blue dress. His brown hair peeked out from under her white lace cap.

"I was wrong to think you would not pass for a daughter of the village, Eric," Wiglaf said.

Eric only nodded.

"That lace cap suits you," Wiglaf went on. "If I were a dragon, I should believe you were a girl—and a fetching one, at that."

"Enough!" Eric snapped. "Keep your thoughts on Gorzil!"

Just then a cloud of smoke billowed out of the cave, and a voice inside boomed, "I SMELL BREAKFAST!"

Wiglaf and Eric hid their swords behind their backs as a huge, green, snakelike head poked out from the smoke. The dragon's eyes blazed orange. Steam rose from his jaws. Yellow slime dripped from his nose. Wiglaf had never seen anything so hideous.

So this was Gorzil! Wiglaf thought back to the minstrel's tale. He gripped his sword more tightly. He hoped that Gorzil would not soon be using Surekill for his toothpick!

Gorzil puffed two smoke rings from his nose. "What luck!" he exclaimed. "Here are a

tasty little son and daughter of the village. And here is Gorzil, hungry for breakfast! Daughter, have you any last words to say to Gorzil?"

Eric took a step forward. He whispered something. But even Wiglaf could not hear what it was.

"What? What?" Gorzil said. "Speak up, girl!" But Eric only whispered again.

The dragon stepped out from the cave. Slime trickled from his nose. It spattered on the ground in greasy yellow puddles. He lowered his head close to Eric. "Now Gorzil can hear better. What did you say, my delicious cookie?"

"I AM NOT YOUR COOKIE, GORZIL!" Eric shouted into the dragon's ear. "I AM YOUR WORST NIGHTMARE!" And he whipped his sword from behind his back.

An angry red crest rose from Gorzil's head.

Sparks shot from his nose. They scorched the hem of Eric's dress. Then Gorzil raised the tip of his tail over his head and whacked Eric's sword out of his hand.

Wiglaf and Eric watched it sail off into the woods.

"Uh-oh," said Eric. He ducked behind a nearby boulder. "Quick, Wiglaf!" he called. "Draw your sword!"

Wiglaf stared up at the monster before him. He tried to remember what he had learned in his one-and-only slaying class. But Gorzil was no dummy dragon with a target painted under his chin. He was the real thing!

With a quivering hand, Wiglaf brought Surekill out from behind his back.

The dragon gazed at the rusty thing and chuckled.

"Surekill," Wiglaf said, "slay the dragon!"

Surekill did not move.

"Surekill!" Wiglaf tried again. "Do the dragon in!"

Surekill made no thrust.

Yellow flames began to flicker from Gorzil's nostrils.

"Surekill!" Wiglaf yelled. "HELP!"

In the blink of an eye, the sword leaped out of Wiglaf's hand. It glowed red hot as it soared up, up into the air. Gorzil stopped flaming. Wiglaf and Eric and the dragon all stared as Surekill rose higher and higher into the clouds. They waited for it to reappear. But the sword had vanished.

At last, Gorzil fixed his gaze back on Wiglaf. "Too bad," he chortled. "Now it is breakfast time!"

Gorzil opened his terrible jaws. Any second, Wiglaf knew, lightning bolts would strike him!

If only I had more time! he thought. *Time*

enough to discover Gorzil's secret weakness! But how? Wiglaf racked his brain. But he could think of nothing. Nothing!

At last, Wiglaf opened his mouth, and over Gorzil's thundering roar, he yelled the first thing that came to his mind: "Knock! Knock!"

Instantly, the thunder stopped.

"A joke!" the dragon cried. "There's nothing Gorzil likes better than a good joke! Breakfast can wait. All right....Who's there?"

"Lettuce," Wiglaf managed.

"Lettuce?" Gorzil snorted a puff of smoke. "Lettuce? Gorzil can guess! Easy! Oh, foo. Lettuce who?"

"Lettuce alone!" Wiglaf answered.

"Oooooh," Gorzil groaned. "That was a bad joke."

"Really bad," Eric called from behind the rock.

"Gorzil *hates* bad jokes," the dragon added.

In fact, Wiglaf thought that the dragon looked slightly ill.

"Try again, son of the village," Gorzil ordered. "Tell Gorzil another joke. But make it a good one!"

"All right," Wiglaf said. "Knock! Knock!"

The dragon perked up. "Gorzil will get this one! Who's there?"

"Arthur!" cried Wiglaf.

"Arthur? Hmm. Oh, yes! Oh, poo. Arthur who?"

Wiglaf answered, "Arthur any dragons uglier than you?"

"Aghh!" Gorzil cried. "That was even worse!"

Wiglaf noticed that Gorzil's bright orange eyes had faded. His scales were no longer a brilliant green. The dragon looked the way Wiglaf felt when he heard too many of Fergus's knock-knocks: Sick.

Suddenly Wiglaf had a hunch. Could it be?

His heart began to race with excitement.

"Knock! Knock!" Wiglaf said again.

"Who's there?" Gorzil mumbled.

"Howard!" called Wiglaf.

"How—Howard who?" Gorzil asked weakly.

Wiglaf yelled, "Howard you like to hear another rotten joke?"

"Another? Uggghh!" The dragon gasped for air. He clutched at his scaly chest with his claws.

Quickly, Wiglaf struck again: "Knock! Knock!"

"Who...there?" Gorzil's head was drooping now.

"Ivan!" Wiglaf shouted.

"Iv...whooo...?" Gorzil's legs buckled under him. He hit the ground.

"Ivan to stay alive!" Wiglaf cried.

That did it. Gorzil's chest heaved. His tail lashed one final time and was still. His tongue flopped out the side of his mouth and lay in a puddle of yellow drool. Then, with a thunderous poof, Gorzil's body exploded into a cloud of dragon dust.

Eric hiked up his skirt and ran through the dust to Wiglaf's side.

"By Lancelot's lance!" he exclaimed. "Gorzil is dead!"

Then all at once, Wiglaf heard a wild roar. He turned to see hundreds of cheering villagers popping out from behind rocks and trees. Villagers who had come to watch them fight the dragon!

Joyfully, the villagers began rushing toward them. Wiglaf brushed the dragon dust from his tunic. He readied himself to be lifted up onto their shoulders. To be carried through Toenail, a hero!

"Out of me way!" a villager shouted gruffly, shoving past him. A stampede of villagers followed on his heels.

Wiglaf and Eric had to leap behind a

boulder or be trampled as the whole crowd charged straight into the cave—straight for Gorzil's hoard.

As the two dragon hunters stood staring, a flash lit the sky. Wiglaf looked up just in time to see Surekill tumble from the clouds—down into a clump of weeds.

"Nice try, Surekill," said Wiglaf.

Chapter 9

"Did the villagers have to grab every last bit of Gorzil's hoard?" Eric grumbled.

By this time, Eric had fetched his sword, and Wiglaf and Eric had found Gawain and Zelda and switched clothes again. Eric told Zelda he was sorry about the burned spots on her dress. But she was so loaded with gold, she did not seem to mind at all.

Now Wiglaf and Eric were back on the path to DSA. This time Eric pulled the cart.

"I am all for taking from the rich and giving to the poor," Eric went on. "But could not the villagers have left us a few gold coins?

How shall we ever face Mordred empty-handed?"

"Gorzil stole from the villagers," Wiglaf reminded him. "It seems only fair that they should get their gold back."

"I suppose," muttered Eric. And with a sigh he dragged the cart over a rocky patch of ground.

"Are you sure you want to pull the cart?" Wiglaf asked him.

"It is the least I can do," Eric told Wiglaf. "For in truth, you did slay the mighty dragon."

Wiglaf blushed on hearing Eric's words. "I could never have done it without you, Eric," he said. "It was a clever plan—and you surely fooled Gorzil into thinking you were a girl."

For a moment, Eric was silent. Then he stopped and turned to Wiglaf. "There is something I should like to tell you," he said gravely.

"Pray, tell," Wiglaf answered.

"'Tis a secret," Eric warned him. "Will you swear to keep it?"

"I swear it on my sword," Wiglaf promised. He lifted Surekill into the air.

"My real name," Eric told him, "is Erica."

"Egad!" Wiglaf exclaimed. "Your parents gave you a girl's name?"

"No! I *am* a girl, you ninny. In fact, I am a princess. Princess Erica, daughter of Queen Barb and King Ken."

Wiglaf's mouth dropped open.

"I always longed for a life of adventure," Erica explained. "When I saw the notice for Dragon Slayers' Academy, I begged my parents to let me go. At last they agreed. But when I arrived at school, Frypot said Mordred would never admit a girl. It was good old Frypot's plan to dress me as a boy.

He keeps my secret. And in return, I empty his eel traps."

"Zounds!" Wiglaf exclaimed. Then he added, "Forgive me, your highness."

"None of that highness stuff!" the princess growled. She drew her silvery sword and waved it at Wiglaf. "You must call me only Eric! And do not slip up! No one at school must know my secret. Not until I get my Dragon Slayers' Academy diploma. If you tell anyone, I shall make you very, very sorry!"

"I shall never say a word," Wiglaf promised. "And if I do, you may tell *my* secret."

"Your secret?" asked Erica.

"See this lucky rag tied to the hilt of my sword?" Wiglaf asked. "It is...uh...the last bit of my baby blanket."

Erica smiled. "Indeed! That is not something that you would want to get around." She gave a yank to the cart handle and started down the path again.

"Now," Erica went on, "let us go over the story we shall tell back at DSA. Since we have no gold, we must make the most of our adventure."

"A fine idea," Wiglaf agreed.

"I think," Erica began, "that we shall start by telling how I bravely lured Gorzil out of his cave. And how I scared him near to death when I brandished my silvery sword! Then, when he least expected it..."

As Eric—make that Erica—talked on, Wiglaf let his own thoughts wander. He had become a hero—just as the minstrel had said he would. And without spilling a single drop of blood!

Daisy would be so proud of me, Wiglaf thought. And wouldn't Fergus and Molwena and his twelve unwashed brothers be surprised when they learned that he was indeed Wiglaf of Pinwick, Dragon Slayer!

DRAGON SLAYERS'
ACADEMY™ 2

REVENGE OF THE DRAGON LADY

KATE McMULLAN

Chapter 1

Wiglaf sat in the cold dining hall of Dragon Slayers' Academy. He stared at the slimy jellied eels on his plate.

"Yuck!" he said to his friend Erica. "I'm sick of having eels for breakfast!"

Erica brushed a clump of brown hair out of her eyes. "Get over it, Wiglaf," she told him.

"I know, I know," Wiglaf said miserably. "The castle moat is swarming with eels. And as long as our headmaster can get eels for free, he will have Frypot cook us eels for breakfast, lunch, and dinner."

With her bread, Erica sopped up every last drop of dark green eel juice on her plate. She popped the bread into her mouth.

How could she stand it? Wiglaf wondered.

"Mmmm," Erica said. "I love it!"

Erica loved everything about DSA—including the eels. She didn't even mind emptying the eel traps each morning. Wiglaf was pretty sure that was one of the reasons she had won the Future Dragon Slayer of the Month Medal.

Wiglaf tasted a small bite of tail. Disgusting! He pushed his plate of eels across the table.

"Here, Erica," he said. "Have mine."

"Shhh! It's *Eric*, remember?" Erica looked around the dining hall to see whether anyone at the other tables had heard. "If Mordred discovers I'm a girl and kicks me out of school, it will be *your* fault!"

"Sorry," Wiglaf said.

"You're the only one who knows my secret," Erica went on. "If you tell anyone, I swear, I'll whack off your head! I'll plunge my sword into your gut! Your blood will—"

"All right, Eric!" Wiglaf cut in quickly. "I get your meaning."

Wiglaf knew Erica was dying to slay a dragon and become a hero. But did she have to go on and on about plunging her sword into *him*?

Wiglaf wanted to be a hero, too. Heroes were brave and bold. If he were a hero, no one would tease him about being small for his age. Or about his carrot-colored hair. So Wiglaf had left home, with his pet pig, Daisy, at his side. He had come to Dragon Slayers' Academy to learn how to kill dragons and become a hero.

There was only one small problem with his plan.

Wiglaf couldn't stand the sight of blood.

"Wiglaf! Eric!" someone called from across the dining hall.

Wiglaf looked up. He saw Angus, the headmaster's nephew, running toward their table.

Angus was plump and sandy-haired. He never ran when he could walk. He never walked when he could sit. So Wiglaf knew he must have important news.

"Angus!" Erica exclaimed. "What is it?"

Angus stood by the Class I table, catching his breath. "Uncle Mordred is having a tantrum," he said.

"That's nothing new," Wiglaf pointed out. Mordred was always yelling at him because of what had happened with a dragon named Gorzil. Wiglaf and Erica had been sent off to kill Gorzil. And Wiglaf *had* killed him. But only by accident. He had stumbled upon Gorzil's secret weakness—bad jokes. And four bad jokes later, Gorzil was history. But Mordred didn't yell about how he had killed the dragon. He yelled about how Wiglaf had let some greedy villagers take all of Gorzil's gold.

"But this is a major tantrum," Angus was saying. "Mordred just heard about a boy from Dragon Exterminators' Prep. He killed a dragon and brought his headmaster all the dragon's gold. Uncle Mordred is screaming and yelling that one of us had better slay a dragon soon.

One of us must bring him some gold, or—"

"Angus!" Wiglaf cried. "Duck!"

Angus ducked. A fat jellied eel flew over his head. It landed in Erica's lap.

Erica leaped to her feet. "Hey! Who threw that?" she called.

"Me!" yelled a boy from the Class II table. "What are you going to do about it?"

"You will see!" Erica yelled back. The Future Dragon Slayer of the Month loved a good food fight as much as any other DSA student. She snatched up an eel from Wiglaf's plate. She threw it. "Bull's-eye!" she yelled as it hit its mark.

At once the air was thick with flying eels.

Wiglaf grinned. Moments like this were the best part of being at Dragon Slayers' Academy! He grabbed an eel. He threw it across the room. Then he joined in the chant that boys at the Class III table had started: "No more eel! No more eel!"

Soon the dining hall was filled with the sound of feet stomping and voices chanting: "No more eel! No more eel!"

Wiglaf picked up the last eel from his plate. He eyed the life-sized bust of Mordred that sat on a post by the door. The headmaster's thick hair, his big popping eyes, and his wide smile had been carved into stone.

Wiglaf took aim. "This one is for you, Mordred!" he yelled. Then he hurled his eel at the stone head.

But at that very moment, the flesh-and-blood headmaster walked through the dining hall door.

Wiglaf stared in horror as his eel hit the real Mordred's face with a mighty splat!

Chapter 2

The eel stuck to Mordred's forehead. Green eel juice dripped into his angry violet eyes. It trickled down his cheeks to his beard.

"You!" Mordred roared at Wiglaf. "I should have known!" He ripped the flattened fish from his forehead. He threw it over his shoulder.

"You!" Mordred thundered. He glared at Wiglaf. "The only DSA pupil ever to slay a dragon! But did you bring me Gorzil's gold? You did NOT!"

"I-I tried to, sir," Wiglaf said. "But the villagers ran into Gorzil's cave, and—"

"Excuses! Excuses!" Mordred shouted. "And

you never paid your tuition! You still owe me seven pennies!"

"That is true," Wiglaf began. "But you see, sir, my family has no money. And my father wanted me to sell my pig. But I—"

"And now you go and hit me with an eel!" Mordred cut in. "As soon as you pay your seven pennies, I shall kick you out of school!"

Mordred took a big red handkerchief from his pocket. He wiped the last of the eel juice from his face.

"But, now," he continued, "it's detention for one and all!" He pointed a fat gold-ringed finger toward the stairs. "To the dungeon! March!"

The DSA students lined up. They marched down three flights of stone steps. One by one, the pupils filed into the cold, damp dungeon.

When everyone was inside, Mordred slammed the door. He lit a pair of torches on the wall.

"Angus! Come here!" the headmaster barked. "The rest of you, sit!"

Angus stepped forward. Wiglaf and the rest of the students sat down on the hard floor.

Mordred gave Angus a jar of quills and several bottles of ink. "Pass these around," he ordered. "Then give out the parchment."

Angus obeyed in silence.

At last everyone had writing supplies.

"Write down all one hundred rules for future dragon slayers," Mordred said. "Neatly, now. No cross-outs or ink blots allowed."

Erica's hand shot up. "Is there a prize for whoever finishes first?" she asked.

"No, Eric. This is a punishment." Mordred frowned at the hourglass he wore strapped to his wrist. "You have two hours. Begin!"

Two hours! Wiglaf's heart sank as he dipped his quill into an ink bottle. He wrote:

100 Rules for Future Dragon Slayers

1. A future dragon slayer will gladly lay

down his life to get gold for Mordred.
2. A future dragon slayer never
complains—especially in letters home.
3. A future dragon slayer eats what is on
his plate—no matter what it looks like.
4. Or tastes like.
5. Or smells like.

Five down, Wiglaf thought. Only ninety-five to go. He glanced over at Erica's paper. How had she written eighteen rules already?

6. A future dragon slayer must keep his
sword sharp and ready for action.

Swords! thought Wiglaf. *That's all anybody at DSA cares about.* He had killed a dragon! So what if he hadn't used his sword. He had done it with jokes. But shouldn't that count for something? It didn't seem to. Nobody seemed to think slaying a dragon with jokes was one bit heroic. Wiglaf sighed. How was he ever going to become a hero?

Wiglaf had just dipped his quill into the ink again when he heard a fluttering noise. He and several others looked up. At the barred window of the dungeon they saw the face of a giant bird!

Mordred looked up, too.

"Zounds!" he yelped. "A bird of evil omen has come to devour us all!"

"My lord!" the bird called. "It is I, your scout, Yorick." He reached out a wing tip and pulled off his big yellow beak. "See?"

"Yorick!" Mordred cried. "Quick! Come down here! Bring me your news!"

A moment later, Yorick waddled into the dungeon. He was covered from head to toe with grimy gray feathers.

"My lord," Yorick said, "I have been spying for you on Buzzard's Peak."

"Ah!" Mordred nodded. "So that explains your buzzard disguise."

Wiglaf thought Yorick looked like a huge pigeon. But he kept his thought to himself.

"My lord," Yorick went on, "a black cloud is blowing in from the east."

Mordred rolled his violet eyes. "I don't pay you to bring me weather reports, Yorick!"

"My lord," Yorick said, "this is no ordinary cloud. It is a cloud of smoke."

"Egad!" Mordred exclaimed. His eyes lit up with excitement. "You cannot mean..."

"I do, my lord," Yorick continued. "A dragon is headed this way. My sources say it is a she-dragon. She is hunting down the warrior who slew her son."

"*Oh!*" Mordred cried. "There is nothing more terrible than an angry mother dragon! I wonder who this unlucky warrior can be?" He tapped his gold-ringed fingers on his chin. "Sir Freddy Headwhacker? No, I'll bet it's that old rascal, Sir Percy Smackbottom."

"My lord," Yorick said, "they say it is the warrior who killed the dragon Gorzil."

"Gorzil?" Angus gasped. "Wiglaf! The dragon is coming after you!"

Chapter 3

iglaf suddenly had a bad feeling in his stomach. And it wasn't from the jellied eel.

"M-m-m-me?" he said.

"You, my boy!" Mordred exclaimed happily. "What luck!"

"Luck?" Wiglaf said. His heart pounded with fear. "It doesn't seem lucky to me."

At this moment, becoming a hero didn't seem so important. Staying alive—that's what mattered.

"Just think—a dragon coming right to my front door!" Mordred smiled. His gold front tooth shone in the torchlight. "Where there's a dragon, there are sure to be piles and piles of

GOLD close by! Oh, just thinking of it boggles the mind!"

"Sir?" Erica called out. "Remember how you sent Wiglaf and me out to kill Gorzil? Well, Wiglaf never even touched that dragon. He killed him by accident!"

"That's true, sir," Wiglaf added quickly.

"See?" Erica said. "Wiglaf even says it's true! But I was ready to kill Gorzil the right way! I had drawn my sword! I was ready to cut off Gorzil's ugly head! By all rights, it's me that Gorzil's mother should be hunting down!"

"Eric," Mordred said patiently, "who turned Gorzil into dragon dust?"

"Well, uh...Wiglaf," Erica admitted. "But—"

Mordred shook a finger at his student. "You must not be jealous of the feats of others," he scolded.

Erica slumped down. "Sorry, sir," she said.

"Are we clear on this?" Mordred asked. "The dragon is after Wiglaf? And Wiglaf alone?"

Wiglaf let out a groan.

"Yes, sir," Erica answered glumly.

"Good." Mordred turned back to his scout. "Yorick," he said, "when will the dragon be here?"

"My lord," Yorick replied, "I multiplied the length of the smoky cloud by its width. Then I subtracted the wind speed—"

"Spit it out, man!" Mordred yelled. "When?"

"My lord," Yorick said, "when the noon bell rings on Friday, Seetha will arrive."

"Friday!" Wiglaf cried. "But that's only two days from—"

"Hush!" Mordred clamped a hand over Wiglaf's mouth. "Yorick! What did you say the dragon's name was?"

"Seetha, my lord," said Yorick.

The smile faded from Mordred's face. "Seetha? The Beast from the East? No!" he wailed. "It can't be! This is too, too horrible!"

Wiglaf started shaking. Seetha must be awful indeed to make Mordred act this way!

"Yorick!" Mordred cried. "I beg you! Say her name is Deetha! Or Queetha! Or Loreetha!"

Yorick only shook his head.

"No dragon has ever come to DSA!" Mordred exclaimed. "Now one is coming. Any dragon in the world would bring along its golden hoard. Any dragon but one. And that one is Seetha!"

"She has no gold?" Angus asked.

"No!" Mordred cried. Tears sprang to his violet eyes. "Seetha cares nothing for gold! All she cares about is killing. She does it for fun!"

"For fun?" Wiglaf squeaked. He started shaking harder. And his teeth began to chatter. "But what does she...How does she..."

"Oh, Seetha loves fun and games," Mordred said. "She plays with her victims for hours before she makes her kill. But she has no gold!" he moaned. "Woe is me! No gold!"

He waved a hand toward the dungeon door. "Go, boys. Detention is over. Just go. Leave me to my sorrow!"

Erica jumped to her feet. "Sir!" she cried. "What you need is a DSA cheer!" She turned to the rest of the students. "Let's do *Look Out, Dragons!* Really yell it now. Ready? And!"

Then everyone—everyone but Wiglaf— marched out of the dungeon shouting:

> "Look out, dragons! Here we come!
> DSA! That's where we're from!
> Will we slay you?
> Yes! We will!
> Here we come to kill! Kill! Kill!"

Chapter 4

"Zorzil's mother is coming to get me!" Wiglaf moaned. He lay on his cot that afternoon during rest hour. "Oh, I'm toast!"

"Pipe down, Wiglaf!" said a tall boy in a cot by the door. "Some of us are trying to rest."

"Go blow your nose, Torblad!" Erica snapped. She sat on the edge of Wiglaf's cot. "I hate to think what you would be like if a dragon was hunting you down!"

Wiglaf moaned louder. He turned to a picture he had drawn of his pig, Daisy, curled up in her cozy bed in the DSA henhouse.

"My poor Daisy!" Wiglaf said. "When I'm gone, she will be all alone in the world."

"That's the least of your worries," Angus offered from his cot on the other side of

Wiglaf's. "Here. This will make you feel better." He broke off a piece of his Camelot Crunch Bar. He handed it to Wiglaf. "Maybe you should run away before Seetha gets here," he added. "Maybe you should go home."

"I can't." Wiglaf passed the candy on to Erica. He was not hungry. "My father told me not to come home without a pile of gold. And he has a temper as bad as Mordred's."

"Uncle Mordred isn't so tough," Angus said. "You should see him when my Aunt Lobelia comes for a visit. She is his big sister. And boy, does she ever boss him around. Once—"

"Angus! Stop talking about your aunt!" Erica broke in. "We have to help Wiggie figure out how he's going to kill Seetha. Look."

Erica reached into her pocket. She brought out two small lead figures. One was a tiny Sir Lancelot. The other was a tiny dragon.

"Here is how *The Sir Lancelot Handbook* says to do it," she said. "'Take up your sword. Smite the dragon on the noggin!'"

Erica made the little Lancelot bonk the little dragon three times on the head.

"*Arrrrgh!*" she wailed. She made the little dragon flop down on its side. "I'm done for!"

"But Seetha won't hold still while I try to smite her!" Wiglaf said. "And let's face it," he added, "I'm no Sir Lancelot."

"I'll say," Erica snorted.

"What you need to do," Angus said, "is find out Seetha's secret weakness. If you can do that, you won't have to smite her."

"I was lucky to have guessed Gorzil's weakness," Wiglaf said. "But what are the chances of that happening again?"

"You don't need luck," Angus said. "You need the right book. There are loads of dragon books in the DSA library."

"What?" Erica exclaimed. "DSA has a library?"

"We have a free period after rest hour," Wiglaf said. "Let's hit the library!"

Chapter 5

BONG! The bell ending rest hour rang.

Angus led Wiglaf and Erica out to the castle yard. Afternoon classes had just begun.

Sir Mort's Stalking Class was learning how to sneak up on a dragon from behind.

Coach Plungett was teaching his Slaying Class the Gut Stab on the practice dragon.

The boys in Frypot's Scrubbing Class were down on their hands and knees washing the castle steps. Mordred claimed that scrubbing was an important skill for future dragon slayers. But Wiglaf never understood exactly why.

The three reached the South Tower. They

ran up a winding stone staircase to the DSA library.

Brother Dave, the librarian, looked up as they walked in. He had a round face and small, round glasses. He wore a brown monk's robe.

"Good day, Angus!" Brother Dave exclaimed. "I see thou hast brought some friends here with thee on this fine afternoon!"

Brother Dave's order of monks had to do good deeds. The deeds had to be so hard that most people could never do them. Brother Dave had decided to become the librarian at DSA, where few of the students—and none of the teachers—had ever read a whole book.

"Art thou here to work on a report that shall keep thee in the library many hours?" Brother Dave asked. He looked hopeful.

"No," Wiglaf replied. "I'm not here about school work...."

"Oh! A child who reads for pleasure!" Brother Dave clasped his hands to his heart. He looked thrilled. "Maybe thou would like

The King Who Couldn't Sleep by Eliza Wake. A great story. Or perhaps thou might try *Into the Dark Forest* by Hugo First. Or, if thou likes poetry—"

"Brother Dave?" Angus cut in. "My friend Wiglaf here is in trouble. He is going to be roasted in two days unless we can get some facts about the dragon Seetha."

"Seetha?" Brother Dave gasped. "Canst thou mean the Beast from the East?"

"You've heard of her, too?" Wiglaf cried. "Oh, please, Brother Dave! I need a book that will tell me Seetha's secret weakness!"

Brother Dave grew thoughtful. "I know of only one book that might tell thee that," he said. "Let me get it." He dashed off and returned with *The Encyclopedia of Dragons*.

Wiglaf gladly took the big book from the monk. Here in his very hands he might be holding the key to Seetha's downfall. Who knew? Perhaps he would live to see Saturday after all!

Wiglaf turned the pages to the "S" section. He kept turning. At last he saw the name *Seetha*. A hideous face stared back at him from the page.

"Whoa!" Angus exclaimed. "That is one scary dragon lady!"

A horn grew out of Seetha's head. Pink curly tentacles sprouted from the base of the horn. They hung down over her yellow eyes. A long tongue curved out of her fang-filled mouth.

"She looks mean, all right," Erica said. "Where do you think you will plunge your sword, Wiggie? Here, in Seetha's neck? Or in her heart? Or maybe in her big, fat gut? Or—"

"Stop!" Wiglaf said. "Let us see what the book has to say."

What it had to say was this:

Full name: *Seetha von Flambé*
Also known as: *The Beast from the East*
Husband: *Fangol von Flambé*
(slain by Sir Gristle McThistle in 943 A.D.)

Children: 3,684

Appearance:

    Scales: swamp green

    Horn: burnt orange

    Eyes: yes

    Teeth: disgusting!

Age: one thousand and counting

Most often heard saying:

    "Let's go torch a wizard's tower!"

Best known for:

    smelling bad...really, REALLY bad

Biggest surprise:

    she's not into gold

Hobby: playing fun killing games

Favorite thing in all the world:

    Son #92, Gorzil, her darling boy

"Oh, I'm doomed!" cried Wiglaf.

"This does not look good for you, Wiggie," Erica said.

The three friends read on. Wiglaf turned the page. Suddenly they all gasped. At the top of the page, it said:

Secret weakness:

Knights who know say Seetha's fatal weakness is ba—

Ink had spilled over the page. The rest of the word was covered with a thick black blob.

"Ba— what?" Wiglaf cried. "I need to know!"

Angus held the page up to the burning candle on Brother Dave's desk. "I can't make out the rest of the word," he said. "But maybe Seetha's weakness is the same as Gorzil's—bad jokes."

Erica shook her head. "No two dragons have the same secret weakness," she said. "I read that in *The Sir Lancelot Handbook*."

"But ba— could be so many things," Angus pointed out. "Bananas. Ballads. Barbecued beef on a bun."

"Looks like you are going to have to slay this dragon the old-fashioned way—with your sword," Erica told Wiglaf. "If I were you, I'd ask Coach Plungett for some extra help in slashing and bashing."

Wiglaf nearly gagged at the thought. "But I'm no good at that stuff!"

"If I were thee," the monk said, gazing down at Wiglaf, "I would start saying my prayers!"

Chapter 6

"Ba— could be bait," Angus said. "Or balloons. Or—"

"We have to go," Erica cut in. "Or we'll be late for Slaying. Thanks, Brother Dave!"

"Ba— could be banjos or back rubs or badminton," Angus went on as they left the library.

"I'm doomed!" Wiglaf exclaimed. "Doomed!"

"Stop being so gloomy!" Erica ordered. "Even if the worst happens, death by dragon is a noble way to die."

"But I don't want to die!" Wiglaf cried.

"Ba— could be baskets," Angus kept on as they ran down the steps. "Or baboons. Or battle-axes."

"It could be a thousand different things," Wiglaf said. "Oh, I wish I could just disappear!"

Angus stopped suddenly.

"Keep moving!" Erica said.

"Disappear," Angus said. He began walking slowly down the steps again. "That gives me an idea. Maybe my Aunt Lobelia could help you, Wiglaf. For there are those who say"— he dropped his voice— "that Lobelia is a sorceress."

"Do *you* think she is?" Wiglaf asked.

Angus nodded. "My mother is always saying that Lobelia can transform people. That she works wonders on them. And you know what?" He smiled. "Mordred keeps a room for Lobelia here in the castle."

Wiglaf stopped dead in his tracks.

"Move!" Erica cried. "You don't want to be late, do you?"

But Wiglaf didn't move. "Angus, do you think Lobelia has something in her room that might transform me?" he asked. "Something to make me disappear for a few days?"

"She might." Angus grinned. "Let's go see. I happen to know that Uncle Mordred keeps the key to her room on a nail over his desk."

"Sneaking in is against DSA rules," Erica reminded them. She fingered her Future Dragon Slayer of the Month Medal which she wore on a ribbon around her neck. "But don't worry," she added. "If you two go, I won't tell. Now, out of my way. I'm going to Slaying." Erica pushed past Wiglaf and Angus. She hurried down the stairs.

Ten minutes later, Angus lifted the latch and slowly opened Mordred's office door. He peeked inside.

"All clear," he whispered.

Wiglaf walked into the office behind Angus. He didn't want to think what the headmaster would do to them if he caught them there.

The boys made their way to the key. They had just reached it when a low moan startled them.

Wiglaf turned. Yikes! There was Mordred! Angus hadn't seen him because he was lying down on his velvet couch.

Mordred had put on a pair of red pajamas. Tears rolled down his cheeks. He was mumbling to himself, "A dragon with no gold. Alas! The thought of it makes me ill!"

Wiglaf sighed with relief. Mordred was suffering far too much to notice them.

Angus lifted the key silently off its nail. Then the boys left the office.

In the hallway, Angus burst out laughing. "What a baby Mordred is!" he exclaimed. "Say, maybe that's Seetha's weakness—babies!"

"Give it up, Angus," Wiglaf said. "We will

never guess Seetha's weakness. I'm pinning my hopes on Aunt Lobelia."

Wiglaf and Angus hurried through dark hallways. At last they came to a wide door in the East Tower. Angus put the key in the lock. *Click!* The door opened.

Wiglaf stepped inside. It was very dark. He swallowed. Maybe breaking into a sorceress's room was not such a good idea. What if it was booby-trapped? What if Lobelia had cast spells against trespassers?

Angus felt his way over to the curtains. He pushed them back. Light flooded in.

Wiglaf looked around. He had expected to see shelves packed with jars of nettles and toadstools. He had very much hoped to see bottles labeled "Invisibility Potion" or "Dragon Repellent."

But instead he saw a fancy sitting room. Dozens of large trunks were lined up against the walls. In the far corner stood a three-sided mirror. Tapestries hung on the walls. Each one showed St. George in some bloody stage of killing a dragon. Wiglaf looked away. Even blood stitched into a tapestry made him sick.

"Maybe she keeps her potions in the trunks." Angus bent down to check one. "It's open," he whispered.

As Wiglaf helped him raise the lid, a husky voice called from the doorway: "Freeze!"

Wiglaf and Angus froze.

"Step away from the trunk," the voice went on. "And I mean *now*!"

Chapter 7

"**T**urn around, you little snoops," the voice said. "Let me have a look at you."

Wiglaf shook with fear as he turned.

"Aunt Lobelia!" Angus exclaimed.

"Angus?" The woman gasped. She dropped her traveling bags. "My stars!"

"I didn't know you were coming for a visit, Auntie," Angus said.

"That's pretty obvious," Lobelia told him.

Wiglaf saw that Angus's Aunt Lobelia had the same thick dark hair as Mordred. She had the same violet eyes, too. But the headmaster was stout. And Lobelia was as thin as a rail.

The sorceress did not look happy. Wiglaf swallowed. What if she turned him into a toad?

A pair of lean hounds with jeweled collars stood at Lobelia's side. The dogs began barking as they, too, recognized Angus.

"Shush, Demon! Lucifer, stop it!" Lobelia said. She threw off a blue velvet cape. Under it, she wore a silvery gown. "So, what are you two after? My jewels?"

"No, Auntie," Angus said. "I'm sorry we broke in. But it's an emergency. This is my friend Wiglaf. He needs help. The dragon Seetha is coming after him!"

"Seetha?" Lobelia cried. "The Beast from the East?"

Wiglaf nodded.

"So it's you she is after! But why?"

"Well, I...um, sort of...by accident, killed her son," Wiglaf explained.

"Bad move," Lobelia said. "On my way here, I passed through the village of Wormbelly. Seetha had just been there. And she left behind her horrible stink." Lobelia wrinkled her nose. "Someone should give that dragon a bottle of perfume. Anyway," she continued, "it seems that Seetha made a mistake. She thought the biggest, strongest man in Wormbelly killed her son. Oh, how she tortured the poor man! She made him play 'Ring Around the Rosie' until he fell down and could not get up."

"Say no more, I beg of you!" Wiglaf cried.

Lobelia shook her head. "Some villagers think he may get his wits back one day. But others fear the worst."

Wiglaf let out a little squeak.

"Seetha will be here at noon on Friday," Angus said. "Can you help Wiglaf, Auntie?"

"Of course I can help," Lobelia answered.

Wiglaf dropped to his knees. "Oh, thank you, Lady Lobelia!" Yes! A sorceress was going to use her magic to help him! Why, he was as good as saved. He grabbed Lobelia's hand and tried to kiss it.

Lobelia yanked her hand away. "Get up!" she ordered. Then she began circling Wiglaf.

She tilted her head. She looked at him from every which way.

"For starters," she said at last, "I'd lose the DSA tunic. And those old breeches. A leather tunic would be nice for you. Brown, to bring out the carrot color of your hair."

Wiglaf had never seen a sorceress at work before. But this was not what he had expected.

Lobelia walked over to her trunks. She started throwing open the lids. From one trunk, she pulled a shirt with billowing sleeves and a pair of quilted yellow breeches. From another, she took brown boots. From still another, forest green leggings and a helmet.

"The ram's horns on this helmet make a strong statement. Don't you think so?" Lobelia asked. "Oh! And this wolf pelt! It's perfect! You can drape it over one shoulder for a sort of Viking effect."

Lobelia piled the clothing into Wiglaf's arms. "Go behind that tapestry and change. We won't peek," she told him. "You know,

Wiglaf, clothes make the man. Or, in your case, the boy. Go on, now! Hurry!"

Wiglaf gave Angus a puzzled look. But he did as he was told. After all, who was he to question the ways of a sorceress?

Wiglaf took off his DSA tunic and his breeches. He put on the shirt. Then he pulled on the green leggings and the heavy yellow breeches. He slipped the leather tunic on over his head. He put on the boots and draped the wolf pelt over his shoulder, Viking style. Finally, he put the ram's-horn helmet on his head. He felt like a fool as he stepped out from behind the tapestry.

Demon and Lucifer began to growl at him.

Angus giggled—until a sharp look from Lobelia made him stop.

"Turn around, Wiglaf," Lobelia ordered. "Let me see the new you!"

Wiglaf turned.

"I am a genius!" Lobelia clapped her hands.

"Seetha will drop *dead* when she sees you!"

"She will?" Wiglaf exclaimed. "For sure?"

"Well, in a manner of speaking," Lobelia answered.

Wiglaf's heart sank. "I didn't think it could be that easy," he said. "But, Lady Lobelia! I need Seetha *really* and *truly* to drop dead! Or she will kill me! Oh, I know you have the power to help me! Angus said—" Wiglaf stopped. He shot a look at his friend.

"Said what?" Lobelia asked. She turned to her nephew. "Angus? Speak up!"

"I said..." Angus mumbled. "I said...uh...that you might be a sorceress."

"A sorceress!" Lobelia's eyes flashed with anger. "Who told you such a thing?"

"My mother," Angus answered.

"What? My own sister?" Lobelia cried.

Angus nodded. "She said that you could transform people. That you worked wonders."

"Oh, now I see." Lobelia smiled. "That part is true enough. I *do* transform people. Have you ever heard of King Richard the Lion-Hearted?"

Wiglaf and Angus nodded.

"Before I fixed him up, you know what people called him?" Lobelia asked. "Chicken-Hearted Richie, that's what! Who do you think put him in the bold red tunic? Who do you think told him to blacken his beard? Me!" Lobelia exclaimed. "Me!

"I transformed that man," she went on. "And I have transformed you, Wiglaf. Listen, if Seetha sees you as a little DSA student, she'll fry you! And from what I hear, she'll take her own sweet time about it, too."

Wiglaf swallowed.

"But," Lobelia went on, "if Seetha sees you as a mighty hero, she'll respect you. And who knows? Maybe she won't even kill you."

"That would be good," Wiglaf said. "Thank you, Lady Lobelia."

Lobelia smiled. "Dress like a hero, Wiglaf, and you *are* a hero. That's my motto!"

Chapter 8

"**S**orry, Wiglaf," Angus said as he and Wiglaf left Lobelia's room.

"Me, too," Wiglaf said. He straightened his ram's-horn helmet. It was so heavy! And the wolf pelt made his neck itch. Worst of all, he didn't believe that the silly clothes would scare Seetha. He wished he had thought to get his clothes back from Lobelia. What would the other boys say when they saw him?

They reached Mordred's office. Angus opened the door and entered the room.

Wiglaf peeked in. He saw that Mordred had fallen asleep.

Angus reached up to put the key back.

But as he did, Mordred's eyes popped open.

"Angus?" he said. "What are you up to?" Then he saw Wiglaf at the door.

"Blazing King Ken's britches!" he yelled. He sat up. "What are *you* supposed to be?"

Wiglaf stepped into the headmaster's office.

"It's...er, a hero look, sir," he said.

"To scare off Seetha," Angus added.

"Bite your tongue, nephew!" Mordred exclaimed. "And never say the name of that no-good, no-gold dragon around me again!"

Mordred mopped his face with his big red hanky. He turned back to Wiglaf. "Where on earth did you ever get such a silly outfit?"

"Lady Lobelia gave me the clothes, sir," Wiglaf answered.

"Oh, Lobelia. That explains it." Mordred nodded. Then his eyes widened in horror. "Egad!" he cried. "Lobelia's *here?*"

"Yes, Uncle," Angus said.

"She never sent word that she was coming," Mordred complained. "I don't suppose she said how long she plans to stay."

Angus shook his head.

"Oh, I'm at death's door already! Five minutes with Lobelia will finish me off!" Mordred exclaimed. "Shoo, boys! Be off! Be gone! Leave me to enjoy what little peace I have left!"

Wiglaf backed away from the miserable headmaster. As he did, he saw a newspaper on Mordred's desk. The headline made Wiglaf's eyes widen in horror.

Wiglaf's hand shook as he picked up *The Medieval Times*. Angus looked over his shoulder. Together they read:

DRAGON LADY HUNTS SLAYER OF SON
Gorzil, Son #92, Was Mama's Darling Boy

RATSWHISKERS, Sept. 32nd
The dragon Seetha von Flambé, also
known as the Beast from the East, is
fighting mad. She and her late husband,
Fangol, had some 3,684 young dragons.
But one little dragon stood out from the
others, and that was Gorzil.

"Gorzil was special," his mother told reporters just before she set fire to East Ratswhiskers yesterday. "When I find the brute who killed him, I don't know what I'll do. But it won't be pretty!"

Lifetime winner of the Stinkiest Dragon Award, Seetha is known as a fun-loving gal. She likes playing games. But when she plays games with her victims, Seetha has all the fun. She brought down Sir Featherbrain by making him do the hokeypokey until he could no longer put his left foot in. She has snuffed out the lives of other brave knights in ways too horrible to mention.

To the warrior who killed Seetha's darling boy, we can only say...Bye-bye!

Wiglaf gulped. He was more scared than he had ever been in his life. Now he almost wished Lobelia had turned him into a toad. At least he would be alive!

Chapter 9

Wiglaf didn't sleep a wink that night. On Thursday morning, he got up, thinking, *This could be the last day of my life!*

Well, he'd do his best to make it a good one.

Wiglaf put on his hero outfit and stuck his sword in his belt. He went to breakfast and ate some scrambled eel. Then he headed for Dragon Science Class with his friends.

"Ba— could be bats," Angus told Wiglaf as they walked. "Vampire bats are pretty scary."

"Maybe it's bandits," Erica put in.

"But Seetha has no gold for bandits to take," Angus said. "Hey! Maybe it's baked beans."

Wiglaf scratched his neck. The mangy wolf

pelt was giving him a nasty rash. He was hardly even listening to Angus and Erica who went on and on about every ba— word under the sun. He knew his friends were only trying to help. But what was the use? Guessing Seetha's secret weakness was impossible!

The three walked into science class.

"Looky! Looky!" Torblad yelled. "Here comes Mr. Puffy Pants!"

Wiglaf tried to look as if he didn't care. All day yesterday, boys had teased him. They said the wolf pelt looked like road kill. They said his helmet had cow horns on it. Every time he went by, they yelled out, "*Moooo!*" But Mr. Puffy Pants. That was even worse!

So much for having a good day.

"Button it up, Torblad!" Erica yelled back. "You *wish* you had puffy pants like Wiglaf's!"

The Dragon Science teacher, tall, thin Dr. Pluck, stood at the front of the room.

"**P**lease sto**p, pup**ils!" Dr. Pluck sputtered.

Dr. Pluck's lips were badly chapped because

he always spit when he said the letter *p*. DSA students made sure they came to Dr. Pluck's class early. They all wanted to get seats in the back rows to keep from getting sprayed.

Wiglaf, Erica, and Angus had not come early. So they took the only empty seats—in the first row.

"**P**lease **p**ay attention, **pup**ils," Dr. Pluck sputtered. He pulled down a large chart of a dragon. All its body parts were labeled. Dr. Pluck put his pointer on the dragon's belly. "The **p**lum**p p**art here is the **p**aunch," he told the class. "Its scientific name is the **pipp**i-hi**pp**o-**papp**a-**peep**us."

Erica's hand shot up. "Can you spell that for us, sir?"

"With **p**leasure," said Dr. Pluck. "**P**-i-**p**-**p**-"

Wiglaf didn't care about spelling right then. He didn't care about parts of a dragon. He didn't even care that Dr. Pluck was spraying him with spit. He stared at the dragon chart.

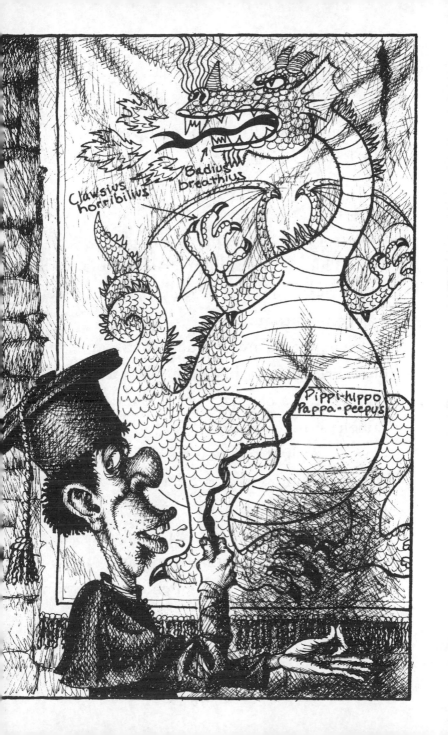

But all he could see was the face of Seetha from Brother Dave's book.

"The **pipp**i-hi**pp**o-**papp**a-**pee**pus," Dr. Pluck went on, "is **p**acked with **p**artly digested **p**ieces of food. **P**ossibly **p**art of a **p**ossum. Or a **p**igeon. **P**lunge a s**p**ear into the dragon's **pipp**i-hi**pp**o-**papp**a-**pee**pus—"

Dr. Pluck showered the class with facts. But Wiglaf was thinking of only one fact. Seetha was coming tomorrow!

Angus would never guess her secret weakness. Erica talked big. But talk was easy. She didn't stand a chance against the dragon. And Lobelia's hero outfit? What a joke! Seetha would see right through his clothes. And then she would know that, under the wolf pelt, he was anything but a hero.

Was there no one to help him?

"In a dragon's **pipp**i-hi**pp**o-**papp**a-**pee**pus," Dr. Pluck was spraying, "might be a **p**ortion of a **p**ig or a—"

Wiglaf suddenly heard Dr. Pluck's words. Pig. Pig. PIG! Yes! Daisy might help him! True, she was a pig. But she was wiser than most people he knew. And, ever since the wizard Zelnoc had put a spell on her, Daisy could speak Pig Latin. Maybe she could tell him how to save himself. Even if she couldn't, Wiglaf wanted to see her. One last time.

So, after Dragon Science, Wiglaf cut Scrubbing. He headed for the henhouse.

"Daisy?" Wiglaf called softly. He didn't want to bother the hens. "Where are you?"

Wiglaf heard the patter of feet on the dirt floor. His pig dashed from her bed. She let out a scream.

Hens fluttered and squawked.

"It's me, Daisy!" Wiglaf exclaimed.

"Iglaf-Way?" Daisy said, backing up.

"Of course it's me." Wiglaf took off the ram's-horn helmet. "See?"

Once Daisy and the hens got used to his

hero look, Wiglaf sat down with his pig. Daisy snuggled up to Wiglaf and listened as he told her about Gorzil's mother.

"Eetha-Say?" Daisy gasped. "E-thay east-bay om-fray e-thay east-yay?"

"Yes. The Beast from the East." Wiglaf nodded sadly. "Her secret weakness begins with ba—. But that is all I know."

In a shaky voice Daisy said, "Acon-bay?"

"Maybe bacon *is* her weakness," Wiglaf said. "But I will never let Seetha get you, Daisy!" He planted a kiss on her snout. "The dragon will be here at noon tomorrow. What shall I do?"

"All-cay Elnoc-Zay," the pig answered.

"The wizard?" Wiglaf said. "But Zelnoc's spells always turn out wrong. He said so himself. He was in for repairs when we met him."

"En-thay oo-whay?" Daisy asked.

"Who, indeed?" Wiglaf thought for a while. "All right, Daisy," he said at last. "I shall call Zelnoc. For even a broken wizard is better than no wizard at all."

Chapter 10

In those days, everyone knew how to call a wizard. All Wiglaf had to do was say Zelnoc's name backwards three times.

Wiglaf wrote on the dirt floor of the henhouse with his finger: Z E L N O C.

Then he wrote it backwards: C O N L E Z.

"Conlez, Conlez, Conlez," Wiglaf chanted.

Suddenly, a tiny bit of smoke appeared. It grew into a smoky, blue pillar. Out of the smoke stepped Zelnoc. He had on a pointed hat and a blue robe covered with stars.

"Bats and blisters!" Zelnoc yelled. "Am I called to a henhouse?" He turned to Wiglaf. "Who are you? Wait! Don't tell me. It's coming to me now. You tried to pull me out of Wizards' Bog. It's Wigwam, right?"

"Wiglaf, sir. Thank you for coming."

"You think I had a choice?" Zelnoc shook his head. "No such thing. When we wizards are called, we show up. Have to. It's Wizard Rule #598."

Now Daisy spoke. "Ello-hay, izard-way."

"Hello, pig! Where in the world did you learn to speak Pig Latin? Oh, I remember. My spell went wrong." Zelnoc sighed. "My spells always do. Well, what can I do for you, Wiglump? Tell me quickly! I want to get back to the Wizards' Convention. Zizmor the Amazing was just starting a demonstration. Oh, what that wizard can do with a few newts' eyes and a drop of bat's blood! And you should see his new wizard's staff. It's a ten-speed model! It casts any spell in half the time."

"I could use a fast spell," Wiglaf said. "For tomorrow, the dragon Seetha is coming to kill me."

"Seetha?" Zelnoc drew back from Wiglaf. "The Pest from the West?"

"No," said Wiglaf. "The Beast from the East."

"Humph," Zelnoc said. "Never heard of that one."

"Well, she's coming to get me," Wiglaf told the wizard. "I'm scared to death! That's why I called you. Can you cast a spell to help me?"

Zelnoc scratched his ear. "A courage spell would fix you up. But can I remember one?"

Zelnoc thought for a minute. Then he snapped his fingers. "Got it! Quick, Wigloaf! Let me say it over you before I forget."

Zelnoc pushed up his sleeves. He stretched out his arms toward Wiglaf. He waggled his fingers.

"Just loosening myself up a bit," the wizard said. "All right. Count to three for me, pig."

"One-yay," said Daisy. "Oo-tway. Ee-thray!"

Zelnoc began to chant:

"Roses are red.

Violets are blue.

Sugar is—"

"Excuse me, sir?" Wiglaf broke in.

"Never stop a wizard midspell!" Zelnoc yelled. "Never!"

"But are you sure that's how a *courage* spell starts?" Wiglaf asked.

Zelnoc thought for a moment. "It doesn't sound right, does it?" He tapped his head with his finger. "Oh, courage spell? Where are you? Ah! There you are! Count again, pig!"

Daisy did: "One-yay. Oo-tway. Ee-thray!"

Zelnoc put one hand on his hip. He bent his other arm and stuck it out to the side. Then he began to sing:

"I'm a little teapot, short and stout!

Here is my handle! Here is my spout!"

"Op-stay, izard-way!" Daisy yelled.

"Sir!" Wiglaf cried. "That can not be it either!"

"Oh, toads and warts!" Zelnoc exclaimed. "I'll call Zizmor. He'll get it right."

Zelnoc shut his eyes and chanted: *"Romziz, Romziz, Romziz!"*

Nothing happened.

He tried again. *"Romziz, Romziz, Romziz!"*

Again, nothing happened.

"Slugs and leeches!" Zelnoc roared. He threw his pointed hat to the ground. He began jumping up and down on it, shouting over and over, *"Romziz! Romziz! Romziz!"*

POOF! Smoke filled the henhouse. Red smoke. Yellow smoke. Bright purple smoke.

The hens sprang from their nests. They raced out of the henhouse, clucking loudly.

"Un-ray, Iglaf-Way!" Daisy yelled.

But Wiglaf stood where he was. He watched in amazement as the smoke swirled into great columns. Out of each column stepped a wizard wearing a gown the color of the smoke. Some two dozen wizards appeared in all. They looked around, muttering.

"Zelnoc?" Wiglaf whispered. "Are these friends of yours?"

"Oh, my stars!" Zelnoc exclaimed. "I've called the whole convention!"

A very tall red-robed wizard with bright red eyes pounded his staff on the floor. The other wizards quieted.

"Did you call me?" the red wizard asked Wiglaf.

"Why...no, sir," Wiglaf said. "You see, Zelnoc thought—"

"Zelnoc!" The red wizard whirled around. "You! I should have known!"

"Sorry, Amazing One," Zelnoc said. He picked up his crumpled hat and stuck it on his head. "I only meant to call you, Ziz. Just you."

Zizmor the Amazing snorted. "Well, what did you want?"

"Tomorrow, this poor boy must fight Seetha," Zelnoc said. He pushed Wiglaf forward.

"Seetha?" Zizmor gasped. "The Beast from the East?"

"Yes, sir," Wiglaf answered.

The lesser wizards whispered darkly among themselves: "Oh, he's a goner. Poor boy. Doesn't stand a chance."

"So," Zelnoc continued, "I said to myself, 'Zelnoc, old sock, old bean, who better to cast a courage spell on this poor lad than Zizmor the Amazing?'"

Zizmor raised an eyebrow. "As it happens, I have been working on a new courage spell. But it's still in the experimental stage."

"I'll try anything!" Wiglaf said. "Please, sir! Can you help me?"

"Does a troll live under a bridge?" Zizmor answered. "Of course I can. And I shall. With pleasure. I would dearly love to take revenge on that fire-breathing beast myself."

"Why is that, sir?" Wiglaf asked.

"Seetha burned down my tower," Zizmor

said. "For no reason. Just flew over, leaned down, and torched it." The Amazing One shook his head. "It's been nothing but carpenters, painters, plumbers, and stonemasons ever since. I hate to think what the final bill is going to be." He closed his red eyes. He breathed deeply to calm himself.

"All right, my boy," Zizmor said, opening his eyes once more. "Are you ready for a dose of courage?"

"I think so, sir," Wiglaf answered.

"I shall give you a double dose," Zizmor said. "No, for Scetha, triple, I think. My triple spell doesn't last too long. But while it's working it's a zinger!"

"Ood-gay uck-lay Iglaf-Way!" Daisy whispered.

Wiglaf waved to his pig. Then he crossed his fingers for luck and got ready for the spell.

Zizmor the Amazing called his fellow wizards to make a circle around Wiglaf. They all stretched out their arms toward him. Zizmor held his ten-speed staff over Wiglaf's head. In a low voice, he chanted:

"Spineless, gutless, weak-kneed brat,
Chicken-hearted scaredy-cat,
Cringing coward, yellow-belly,
Lily-livered, heart of jelly.
Change this boy who's standing here,
Into He-Who-Knows-No-Fear!"

Sparks began to fly from Zizmor's staff.

Wiglaf gasped as they showered down on him. *Ziz! Ziz! Ziz!* The sparks flashed and popped. The roar of rushing wind filled Wiglaf's ears. And then the wizards began to swirl before his eyes.

The next thing Wiglaf knew, he was lying on the henhouse floor.

All the wizards stared down at him.

Zelnoc's face appeared close to Wiglaf's. "Speak to me, lad!" he cried. "Speak to me!"

Chapter 11

"Where is Seetha?" Wiglaf growled. He leaped to his feet. "Where is that ugly dragon?"

"Uh—thought you said she was coming tomorrow," Zelnoc said.

"I can't wait until tomorrow!" Wiglaf exclaimed.

He snatched his ram's-horn helmet from the floor. He jammed it on his head. "I shall save the world from the Beast from the East today! First, I shall slash Seetha's throat!" He drew his sword and sliced at the air. "Then I shall stab her through the heart!" He lunged forward, shouting, "Take *that*, you scaly scavenger!"

"Oh, dear," Zelnoc said. "Maybe the triple spell was a little much, Ziz."

"Fiddlesticks," Zizmor scoffed. "All right, fellow enchanters!" he called to the other wizards. "Clearly our work here is finished. Let's get back to the convention, shall we? I believe there's a brew-tasting party tonight."

"Wait for me, Ziz!" Zelnoc said. "Good luck, Wigloop!"

"Luck? Who needs luck?" Wiglaf exclaimed. "Not I! For I have courage!"

"Oh, dear," Zelnoc said again as smoke began to fill the henhouse.

Ten seconds later, both the smoke and the wizards had disappeared.

Wiglaf charged out of the henhouse. He waved his sword and shouted:

"Look out, Seetha! Here I come!
DSA ! That's where I'm from!
Will I slay you?
Yes! I will!
Here I come to kill! Kill! Kill!"

Daisy ran to the henhouse door. She called after him, "Ait-way, Iglaf-Way!"

"Sorry, pork chop," Wiglaf called back. "I have a dragon to slay!"

He-Who-Knows-No-Fear marched across the castle yard. From the tips of the ram's horns on his helmet down to the toes of his new boots, every inch of him was filled with courage. There was only one thing he wanted—action!

"Seetha's a fun-loving dragon, is she?" Wiglaf growled. "Well! Let's see how much fun she has when I stab her in the pippi-hippo-pappa-peepus!"

Wiglaf saw that Sir Mort had brought the Class I students out to the castle steps. They were having a Rubbish Relay. This was a scheme of Mordred's for getting the litter in the castle yard picked up.

"Wiglaf!" Erica called. "We were looking for you!" She and Angus broke away from the group. They ran up to him.

Angus waved a piece of parchment. "I've started a ba— list. I'll find Seetha's weakness yet! Listen—bald men, ballet dancers, bank robbers, barbers, baton twirlers, barking dogs—"

"Stop!" Wiglaf yelled. "What care I for Seetha's weakness? I shall slay her with my sword!"

Erica's eyes grew wide. "Wiglaf! You don't sound like yourself. Where are you going, anyway?"

"I am off to find the Beast from the East!" Wiglaf exclaimed. "I'll not wait for her to hunt me down. Nay! I shall hunt *her* down! I shall cut that dragon into a thousand pieces!"

"All *right*, Wiggie!" Erica punched her fist in the air. "You speak like a true dragon slayer at last!"

Wiglaf squared his shoulders. He marched through the gatehouse. He started across the drawbridge. Erica and Angus had to run to keep up with him.

"Look!" Angus yelled. He stopped suddenly. "Some strange creature is coming!"

"Creature?" Wiglaf drew his sword. "Never fear! I shall protect you!"

He looked where Angus was pointing. A giant rabbit was hopping toward the drawbridge.

"Run!" the rabbit screamed as it hopped. "Run for your lives!"

Wiglaf stuck his sword back in his belt. It would not do to slay such a helpless creature.

"You heard the rabbit!" Angus cried. "Quick! Into the castle!" He grabbed Wiglaf by the wolf pelt. He tried to drag him back toward the gatehouse.

"Unhand me, man!" Wiglaf cried. He struggled with Angus.

The rabbit hopped closer. Wiglaf saw that it wasn't a rabbit at all. It was a man in a bunny suit.

Erica eyed the rabbit. "Yorick?" she said. "Is that you?"

"It's me," the rabbit said. "I have come to say I was wrong. Seetha won't be here at noon on

Friday. You see, I should have multiplied the wind speed by the width of the smoke cloud. Then divided—"

"Out with it, Yorick!" Wiglaf roared.

"Seetha will be here at noon on *Thursday*," Yorick told them.

"But today is Thursday!" Angus pointed out. "And it's almost noon!"

"Right," Yorick said. "And guess what? Seetha is here!"

Chapter 12

Wiglaf raised his eyes to the sky. Far away, he saw a small, dark cloud. He sniffed the air. Pew! It smelled like rotten eggs.

Wiglaf centered his ram's-horn helmet. He brushed off his wolf pelt. He drew his sword. Then he struck a manly pose on the drawbridge.

"Seetha, you have but little time to live!" Wiglaf roared at the sky. "For I was born to slay you!"

Yorick backed slowly away from Wiglaf. Then he turned and ran across the drawbridge as fast as the legs of his bunny suit would allow. "She's here!" he yelled. "Seetha's here!"

Mordred stuck his head out a tower window. "Seetha's here?" he cried. "Egad!"

"Seetha comes to meet her doom!" Wiglaf called up to the headmaster. "That's me," he added. "*I* am her doom!"

"Oh, right." Mordred rolled his violet eyes. Then he stuck a whistle in his mouth. He blew it until his face was as red as his pajamas, which he still had on.

"Everybody into the castle!" he called. "Hurry now! Step on it, Angus! You, too, Eric!"

"No!" Erica called back. "I shall stay and fight the dragon!"

"Me, too, I guess," said Angus.

Wiglaf looked up. The dark cloud was blowing quickly toward DSA.

"Angus!" Mordred yelled. "Get inside! Do you know what your mother would do to me if I let a dragon get you?"

"Sorry, Wiglaf." Angus shrugged. Then he ran into the castle with surprising speed.

The dark cloud began to drop. Wiglaf saw green smoke puff out from its edges. But its middle was as dark as midnight.

"You, too, Eric!" Mordred yelled. "Inside!"

"No, sir!" Erica cried. "I must fight beside Wiglaf!"

The cloud dropped lower. The smell of rotten eggs grew stronger.

"Into the castle!" Mordred roared. "Now!"

Thunder rumbled from inside the cloud.

"Never!" Erica cried. "I shall not leave my friend in battle! That's Dragon Slayers' Rule #37!"

Once more Mordred's face began to turn as red as his pajamas.

"I *order* you into the castle!" he yelled. "Get in here now! Or turn in the Dragon Slayer of the Month Medal."

Erica gasped. She clutched at her medal.

"Do as he says!" Wiglaf told her. "Seetha is my dragon! This is my fight!"

Erica looked from Wiglaf to Mordred and

back to Wiglaf. "Oh, all right," she said at last. "But take this." She put a small, pointy dagger into Wiglaf's hand. "It's from *The Sir Lancelot Catalog.* It's called Stinger. Good luck, Wiggie!"

So saying, Erica walked sadly across the drawbridge. Wiglaf stuck the dagger into his boot. He stood alone outside the castle. The smoky, smelly, rumbling cloud stopped right over DSA.

"I'm waiting for you, Seetha!" Wiglaf yelled.

The cloud began to drop. Then out of the smoke poked the ugly head of Seetha. Her yellow eyes glowed. Her long tongue flicked out of her mouth. "WAIT NO MORE!" she cried.

Wiglaf gagged as the dragon's breath hit him. It smelled like a garbage dump come to life.

Seetha spread her wings. She flew down from her cloud. She landed beside the moat.

Her smell landed with her. Wiglaf almost

wished Zizmor had changed him into He-Who-Smells-No-Foul-Odors. Seetha was one stinky dragon!

"I AM SEETHA!" the dragon roared. "WHOEVER KILLED MY DARLING BOY— PREPARE TO DIE!"

Chapter 13

"I killed Gorzil!" He-Who-Knows-No-Fear shouted to the dragon.

"YOU?" Seetha drew her lips back from her pointy teeth in what Wiglaf guessed was a smile. "YOU ARE NOT BIG ENOUGH TO KILL A FLEA!"

"I did the deed," Wiglaf yelled. "Me! Wiglaf of Pinwick, Dragon Slayer!"

"THEN TELL ME, WIGLAF, HOW DID GORZIL DIE? LAUGHING AT YOUR SILLY CLOTHES?"

"He died laughing," Wiglaf answered. "Laughing at some jokes I told him. Bad jokes. *Really* bad."

"OH!" Seetha gasped. "YOU GUESSED

HIS SECRET WEAKNESS!" Large orange tears oozed out of her eyes. They rolled down her scaly cheeks. She sniffed. "MY GORZIE WAS EVERYTHING A YOUNG DRAGON SHOULD BE!" she cried. "THE DARLING BOY WAS GREEDY! LAZY! RUDE! CRUEL! HE CHEATED EVERY CHANCE HE GOT! HE WAS...PERFECT!"

Seetha swiped a claw across her runny nose.

"BUT ENOUGH CHIT-CHAT!"she roared. "IT'S PAYBACK TIME!"

Seetha flew up and landed on the castle wall. She looked around. Her eyes found Coach Plungett's practice dragon in the castle yard.

"LET ME GIVE YOU A LITTLE DEMON-STRATION! HERE'S A GAME YOU AND I MIGHT PLAY, WIGLAF!" Seetha exclaimed. "SPIT BALL!"

She made a hacking sound in the back of her throat. Up came a blob of fire. She spit it at the straw dragon. WHOOSH! It burst into flames.

Mordred poked his head out of the tower

window. He cupped his hands to his mouth.

"Excuse me, dragon lady, ma'am?" he called.

Seetha turned toward the window. "AND YOU WOULD BE..."

"Mordred, Your Scaliness. I'm Headmaster of Dragon Sla...um, of this school." He bowed. "Go ahead and have your fun with the boy. But, please. Try not to set the school on fire. I'm afraid that if a spark hits the—"

Seetha cut him off by spitting a fire ball at his head. The headmaster quickly disappeared from the window.

Seetha flew back down to the grass near Wiglaf. "NOW...HOW SHALL I DO YOU IN?" She tapped a claw on her scales, thinking. "WE COULD PLAY BADMINTON—WITH YOU AS THE BIRDIE."

"Whatever, Seetha!" Wiglaf growled. "But I swear by the ram's horns on my helmet that *you* shall be the one to die!" He waved his sword in the air. And with a mighty battle cry he charged at the beast.

Seetha's eyes widened with surprise. Then she blew a puff of red-hot dragon breath right at Wiglaf.

The blast of smelly heat almost knocked Wiglaf off his feet. His wolf pelt crackled. It curled at the edges. Sweat popped out on his brow. But still he ran toward the dragon.

With one claw, Seetha knocked the sword out of Wiglaf's hand. With the other, she struck him. He went rolling head over heels.

Wiglaf came to a stop near the edge of the moat. Before he could get back on his feet, Seetha struck again. She hooked Wiglaf's wolf pelt with her claw. She lifted him up off the ground.

Wiglaf swayed crazily in the air as the dragon lifted him higher and higher. Soon he was face to face with Gorzil's awful mother.

"Back off, smelly one!" Wiglaf cried. "A thousands skunks are not as stinky as you."

Seetha smiled. "Thank you," she said.

Wiglaf was only inches from Seetha's face.

He saw that her scales were covered with dirt and scum. A crust of old, dried slime coated her nose. Her moss-covered fangs had holes in them the size of dinner plates.

"HMMMM...WHAT'S THE *WORST* WAY FOR YOU TO DIE?" Seetha said. "I KNOW! THE TICKLE TORTURE! YOU'LL DIE LAUGHING—JUST LIKE MY GORZIE!"

"Not me!" cried He-Who-Knows-No-Fear. "I can take it!" The dragon's dirty claw came closer and closer to him.

"KITCHY-KITCHY-KOO!" Seetha cried. She tickled Wiglaf's tummy. His neck. His armpits. "KITCHY-KITCHY-KOO!"

But Wiglaf never even smiled.

"NO FAIR! YOU'RE NOT TICKLISH!" Seetha pouted for a minute. "BUT I KNOW MORE GAMES. MANY MORE! LET'S PLAY 'HIGH DIVE'!"

Still clutching Wiglaf, Seetha spread her wings and took off. She landed on the gatehouse roof. She held Wiglaf out, over the moat. "CAN YOU DO A JACKKNIFE WITH A HALF TWIST? HMMMMM?"

Wiglaf looked down. Hundreds of eels looked up at him. They hungrily snapped their jaws.

"You can't scare me, Seetha!" Wiglaf yelled. He drew Erica's dagger from his boot. "For I am He-Who-Knows-No-Fear!"

"OH, YEAH?" the dragon roared. "WELL, I AM SHE-WHO-MAKES-BRAVE-KNIGHTS-CRY-LIKE-BABIES!"

Wiglaf opened his mouth to reply. But a dizzy feeling swept over him. Bright lights flashed. He heard the rush of wind. Seetha's face seemed to melt.

He squeezed his eyes shut.

When he opened them again, the courage spell was broken.

He-Who-Knows-No-Fear was gone.

Now, caught in the dragon's claw was plain old Chicken-Hearted Wiglaf.

Chapter 14

"*Yiiiiiiiiiiiiiiiiiiiiiiiii!*" screamed Wiglaf. His heart thumped with terror. Any second, Seetha would roast him! Or toast him! Or feed him to the eels!

He tried covering his eyes with his hands. But...what was *this* in his hand?

"MAYBE YOU SHOULD TRY A DOUBLE SOMERSAULT!" Seetha roared. She dangled Wiglaf further out over the moat.

Wiglaf didn't answer. He stared at the dagger. What a sharp, sharp point it had. He could stab Seetha with it. But the very thought made him feel sick. With a shudder, Wiglaf let the dagger slip from his hand.

"*OW*!" Seetha yelped as Stinger stuck her. "MY TOE! MY BEAUTIFUL BIG TOE! WHAT HAVE YOU DONE?"

Seetha tossed Wiglaf away. He sailed through the air. With a thump, he landed on the ground. He bounced twice. Then he lay still.

Above him, the dragon howled in pain. "MY FAVORITE TOE! IT'S BLEEDING!"

Wiglaf moaned. He would be bruised all over. But thanks to Lobelia's heavy leather tunic and thick, quilted breeches, he would live. He pulled himself slowly to his feet.

The dragon rocked back and forth on the gatehouse roof. "LET ME KISS YOU AND MAKE YOU ALL BETTER!" she said to her toe.

Wiglaf glanced up. Seetha held her hurt foot in her front claws. She puckered up her purple lips. With a loud SMACK! she planted a kiss on her toe.

Then Seetha began hopping up and down on her good foot. "I'LL GET YOU, WIGLAF!" she roared. "I'LL MAKE YOU SIZZLE LIKE A FRENCH FRY!"

Wiglaf groaned.

He was a goner!

So Wiglaf did what any chicken hearted boy would do. He crouched down. He covered his eyes and shook with fear.

"HERE I COME!" Seetha screamed. "I'LL...WHOA! HEY! WHOOO!"

Wiglaf peeked out from behind his fingers.

Seetha teetered on the roof above him. She still held her hurt toe. But something was wrong. Her wings flapped clumsily. Her tail lashed the air. She swayed dangerously back and forth. She lost her balance. Down she plunged.

SPLASH!

Seetha hit the moat.

A huge cloud of steam rose from the waters.

Wiglaf couldn't see a thing.

Suddenly, the dragon lurched up, out of the mist.

Wiglaf jumped back.

"HELP!" Seetha screamed. "HELP ME, YOU FOOLISH BOY!"

But Wiglaf was not *that* foolish.

Seetha kicked and splashed. She slapped the water with her tail.

Wiglaf saw that Seetha's scales looked clean but dull. Her yellow eyes had faded, too. Her horn was drooping to one side. Her tongue hung out the side of her mouth.

"I CAN'T TAKE THIS MUCH LONGER!" Seetha cried. "HELP ME! I'LL GIVE YOU HEAPS OF GOLD!"

Before Wiglaf could shake his head *no*, Mordred leaned out the castle window. "Gold?" he called. "But everyone knows that you have no gold, Seetha!"

"HA!" Seetha laughed. "THAT OLD RUMOR? I'VE GOT MORE GOLD THAN

ANY TEN DRAGONS PUT TOGETHER! AND I HID IT ALL IN THE DARK FOOOOLUB—"

She disappeared under the water again.

Suddenly the drawbridge came down with a bang.

Mordred zoomed out of the castle. He pushed Wiglaf out of the way. He dropped to his knees.

"Seetha!" he cried. "Madam Seetha! Can you hear me?"

"GLUG-GOLD!" Seetha sputtered, popping up. "GET ME OUT OF HERE, BIG BOY— AND IT'S YOURS!"

"Mine?" Mordred gasped as Seetha sank. "Come back, Madam! We have to talk!"

Only Seetha's purple lips popped up now. "GOLBLUB....GLOOOOPH!" The dragon belched and disappeared.

"Hold on, Seetha!" Mordred cried. "I'll save you!" And the headmaster of Dragon Slayers'

Academy dove into the moat to rescue the dragon.

Wiglaf stood alone on the drawbridge. He watched Mordred dive down to find the dragon.

But it was no use.

Seetha's head never again appeared above the dark and murky waters of the moat.

But Mordred's did. "Dragons don't drown!" he cried at last. "How can this be happening?"

Suddenly Wiglaf knew the answer.

"Seetha died from her secret weakness!" he called to the soggy headmaster. "It was a *bath* that killed the beast!"

Wiglaf straightened his ram's-horn helmet.

Then, with his head held high, he walked across the drawbridge and back to DSA.

Mordred stood before all the DSA students in the dining hall that night.

"Did Wiglaf ask Seetha about her gold?" he asked in a hoarse voice.

"Nooooo!" Mordred answered himself. "So I have none of it! Not a single gold coin! All I have—" he sneezed loudly into his red hanky "—is double pneumonia!"

Mordred covered his face with his hands. He began to cry.

"I have some bad news, too," Frypot told the students. The cook made his way to the front of the room.

"When Seetha fell into the moat," he continued, "that filthy dragon poisoned the eels! She killed every single one of them dead."

"What?" Mordred lifted his tear-stained face. "You mean now I have to *buy* groceries to feed all these little gluttons? Oh, this *is* cruel!"

"I'm sorry to tell you this, boys," Frypot went on. "But your days of eating my yummy eel dishes are over."

A hush fell over the great hall.

Then all the students jumped to their feet. They began clapping and stomping and whistling.

Angus shot Wiglaf a thumbs-up sign. "Let's give a cheer for Wiglaf!" he cried.

And they all began to shout. Even Erica, the only DSA student who would actually miss Frypot's eels:

> *"No more eel! No more eel!*
> *Never again for any meal!*
> *Wiglaf! Wiglaf! He's our man!*
> *If he can do it, anybody can!*
> *Yeaaaaaaaaaa Wiglaf!"*

The students kept clapping and cheering. It warmed Wiglaf's heart. Maybe he hadn't killed Seetha with his sword. Maybe his courage had come from a wizard's spell. But tonight in the DSA dining hall, he was certainly a hero.

DRAGON SLAYERS' ACADEMY™ 3

CLASS TRIP TO THE CAVE OF DOOM

KATE McMULLAN

Chapter 1

link! Clink! Clink! Mordred, the headmaster of Dragon Slayers' Academy, banged his spoon on his glass. *Clink! Clink! Clink!*

"Boys!" Mordred's loud voice filled the DSA dining hall. "I have a surprise for you!"

Egad! thought Wiglaf. *What now?* Mordred's last surprise had been a scrubbing party. Wiglaf had been up half the night, working on the stew pot.

"Maybe Uncle Mordred caught the boys who threw his boots into the moat," Angus whispered to Wiglaf. Angus was the headmaster's nephew. But Wiglaf didn't hold that against him. "Or maybe," Angus went on, "he found out who dropped Sir Mort's false teeth into the cider jug."

"Shh, Angus!" said Erica, who was also Wiglaf's friend. "We're supposed to be—"

"QUIIIIIET!" Mordred roared.

A hush fell over the dining hall.

"That's better." The headmaster smiled. His gold tooth shone in the torchlight. "Now, as you know, Wiglaf has killed two dragons."

Wiglaf gasped. Could it be? Was Mordred at last going to honor him as a hero?

"But tell me, boys," Mordred continued. "Did Wiglaf bring back any dragon gold for *me?*"

"Nooooooo!" the DSA students cried.

Wiglaf slid down in his seat. He should have known! Mordred was only picking on him—again.

Wiglaf was sick of being picked on. Back home, his twelve brothers picked on him all the time. They called him Runt, because he was small for his age. They made fun of his carrot-colored hair and his pet pig, Daisy. They teased him about his tender-hearted ways.

Wiglaf had hoped that things would be better at school. He had come to DSA to learn to be a hero. And he *had* killed two dragons. A young one named Gorzil and his mother, Seetha. But the truth was, Wiglaf had killed them by accident. He could never have cut off their heads. Or poked his sword into their guts. The very thought of blood made Wiglaf sick to his stomach. Still, he *had* killed them. That should count for something. And he was the only boy at DSA ever to kill *any* dragon. But Mordred didn't care about dead dragons. All he cared about was getting his hands on their gold.

"Wiglaf brought me no gold," Mordred moaned softly. "No gold." Then his violet eyes lit up. "But rumors are flying!" he exclaimed. "Villagers in Ratswhiskers say that before Seetha died, she hid all her gold in a cave in the Dark Forest."

Erica jumped up. "Let *me* go to that cave, sir!" she cried. "I shall bring you Seetha's gold!"

Wiglaf smiled. Erica was so gung ho about dragon slaying. Mordred did not let girls into his school. So Erica cut her straight brown hair and dressed as a boy so she could go to DSA. Everyone there called her Eric. Only Wiglaf knew that she was really Erica. Princess Erica, as a matter of fact.

"You *shall* go, Eric," Mordred roared. "*All* of you are going on a class trip to the Dark Forest! That is my surprise! All of you are going to hunt for Seetha's gold!"

"Hooray!" Erica cried.

A few others cheered. But not Wiglaf. The

Dark Forest was not exactly a vacation spot. It was *dark*, for one thing. And very scary.

"You shall meet in the castle yard tomorrow morning," Mordred continued. "Then you shall march into the Dark Forest. And the boy who finds Seetha's gold..." Mordred rubbed his hands together. "...will get a great big *prize!*"

"Hooray!" everyone cheered this time.

"Wiggie!" Erica called over the cheering. "I am sure to find Seetha's gold, so you and Angus stick with me. That way, you can share the prize!"

Wiglaf nodded. If only the prize were some of Seetha's gold. Then he could pay the seven pennies he still owed DSA for his tuition. He could send some money to his greedy family back in Pinwick. And maybe—just maybe—if he found Seetha's gold, Mordred would stop picking on him.

Chapter 2

"**J**ump, boys! Higher!" Coach Plungett, the DSA slaying teacher, called early the next morning. His brown pageboy wig blew in the breeze as he counted jumping jacks. "Ninety-one! Ninety-two! Exercise will make you manly men, like me!"

Wiglaf had never done so many jumping jacks. His arms were ready to drop off.

But Coach kept counting. "One hundred three!" he cried. "Jumping is a manly way to warm up on a chilly morning!"

The boys had stumbled into the castle yard

before sunup. Coach Plungett put them into groups. Coach was the leader of the Bloodhounds. Wiglaf was a Bloodhound. Angus and Erica were Bloodhounds, too. So were the big Marley brothers: Barley, Charlie, Farley, and Harley.

Wiglaf looked over at the Marleys doing sloppy jumping jacks. He couldn't tell one brother from another. They never said much. They were known for playing jokes. Wiglaf was pretty sure the Marleys had thrown Mordred's boots into the moat.

"One hundred twenty!" Coach counted.

"I cannot...do any...more!" Wiglaf gasped.

"This is nothing," yelled Erica. She was jumping next to him. "I once did six hundred jumping jacks. And I wasn't even out of breath."

Wiglaf could barely hear what Erica was saying. Her tool belt was clanking too loudly.

She had sent away for it from the Sir Lancelot Fan Club catalog. All sorts of fine dragon-slaying equipment hung from the wide silver belt. A canteen. A collapsible goblet. A spyglass. A magnifying glass. A rope. A small copy of *The Sir Lancelot Handbook*. A mini-torch. A pack of dry sticks for starting fires. A spare sword. A lice comb. And a toothpick.

All Wiglaf had was a beat-up sword. His lucky rag was tied to the handle. But now, as he did his one hundred eighty-second jumping jack, he was just as glad not to be wearing a heavy tool belt.

"Where is Mordred anyway?" Erica asked.

"You know Uncle Mordred hates to get up before noon," Angus answered.

Angus moved his arms up and down as Coach counted. But he kept his feet planted on the ground. Since Angus was Mordred's nephew, Coach Plungett pretended not to notice.

"Two hundred!" Coach called. "Halt!"

Wiglaf stopped jumping. He thought *halt* was the most beautiful word he'd ever heard.

"Now hit the ground for two hundred push-ups!" Coach called.

Wiglaf groaned. Was Coach trying to slay them?

Luckily, at that moment, the castle door opened. Mordred stepped outside. He raised a megaphone to his mouth. He called, "Atten*tion!*"

The boys snapped up straight and tall.

"Each group leader has a map of part of the Dark Forest," Mordred went on. "Each map shows all the caves in that part. Look in every cave, boys. There's gold in one of them!"

"The Bloodhounds shall find it!" Erica cried.

"Nay!" a boy called out. "The Bulldogs!"

"No! The Wolfhounds!" called another boy.

"Wrong!" another piped up. "The Poodles!"

"That's the spirit, boys!" Mordred cried. He walked down the castle steps. Six skinny DSA student teachers hurried over to him. They carried a large throne-like chair with poles attached to its seat. The student teachers lowered the chair. Mordred sat down in it.

"They're going to *carry* him?" Wiglaf exclaimed.

"You didn't think Uncle Mordred would walk to the Dark Forest, did you?" Angus asked.

"No monkeying around," Mordred called. "I'll come check on you from my camp." He gave a signal. Four student teachers picked up his chair. The others picked up his camping gear. Wiglaf saw that it included pillows, thick blankets, and red pajamas with feet.

Tweeeeeeeeeeeeeeeeeeet! Mordred gave a blast on his silver whistle. They were off!

Coach led the Bloodhounds across the castle yard. Everyone carried a heavy pack. The

big Marley brothers carried theirs with ease. Wiglaf staggered under his as he marched over the DSA drawbridge.

Wiglaf looked down into the castle moat. How well he remembered Seetha splashing in its waters before she went down for the last time. The secret of where she hid her dragon gold had gone down with her. Now, he was off to hunt for that gold. And, by St. George, he was going to find it!

The Bloodhounds marched up Huntsman's Path. They marched through Vulture Valley. They marched around Leech Lake. And across Swamp River Ridge.

"Halt!" Coach ordered at last.

Wiglaf stopped. There was that lovely word *halt* again. He gladly dropped his pack to the ground.

Coach took out his map. He looked at it for a long time. "We are now in the south part of the Dark Forest," he said. Then he frowned.

He turned the map upside down. "Or are we in the north part?"

Wiglaf and Angus looked over Coach's shoulder.

"Zounds!" Wiglaf cried. "There must be a hundred caves on that map!"

"We'll be marching around here forever!" Angus said. "Let's give up and go home."

"Bloodhounds never give up!" Erica cried.

"That's the way, Eric!" Coach said. "All right, Bloodhounds. On your feet."

The Bloodhounds picked up their packs. They started off. The Marleys marched behind Wiglaf. They began a contest to see which one of them could burp the loudest. Wiglaf thought they all should get first prize.

"Coach?" Erica called out. "I made up a Bloodhound marching song."

"Good work!" Coach cried. "Why don't we sing it as we march?"

Erica sang her song through once. Then all

the Bloodhounds marched through the Dark Forest, singing:

"We're the mighty Bloodhounds!
We're dogged and we're bold!
We're the mighty Bloodhounds!
We'll track down Seetha's gold!
We'll put our noses to the ground!
We'll give a mighty sniff!
Will we ever loose the scent?
No! No! Not us! As if!
'Cause...we're the mighty Bloodhounds!
Hear us when we yell!
We're the mighty Bloodhounds!
And do we ever smell!"

The Bloodhounds looked in twelve caves that morning. Most were empty. But not all. The Cave of Really-Loud-Snoring housed a family of sleeping bears. Cave Hole-in-the-Roof was full of puddles. And Jolly-Good-

Times Cave was piled high with old mead flasks.

Inside Jolly-Good-Times Cave, the Marleys started yelling and whooping and picking up the flasks. They shook them upside down over their mouths. They were hoping for a drop or two of mead, but the flasks were empty.

"Charlie!" cried Coach. "Parley! Whatever your names are! Cut that out!"

He lined everyone up again. Off they marched down Snakes' Path.

"Say, my manly men!" Coach called as they marched. "Who is going to find the gold?"

"The Bloodhounds!" Erica yelled.

Wiglaf hoped Erica was right. That would make all his pain worthwhile. The heavy pack hurt his back. He had blisters on every toe. He was hungry. And it wasn't easy keeping up with Erica.

At a bend in the road, Wiglaf heard a low growl.

"Is that your stomach?" he asked Erica.

"No," she said. "I thought it was yours."

The growling grew louder.

Suddenly a wild man leaped out at them! He had thick white hair. His beard hung down to his knees. He swung a pointed stick over his head and charged at the Bloodhounds!

Chapter 3

iglaf ran behind a tree for cover. The Marleys hid behind a big rock. Angus hid behind Wiglaf.

Erica stood her ground beside Coach.

The wild man shook his stick. "Danger!" he cried. "Do not go to the Cave of Doom!"

"Doom?" Wiglaf whispered. "Did he say *doom?*"

"I think so," Angus whispered back. "I'm not going into any cave called Doom."

"Danger!" the hermit cried again. "Do not pass go! Do not stick rocks up your nose!"

"Be gone!" Coach called with a toss of his

head, which made his wig slide to the left.

"First hear my tale!" the hermit cried. "It's a sad tale. Nothing like a fish tail. More like a pig tail. Kind of twisty..."

"Get on with it!" Coach ordered.

"Seven brave men followed me into the Cave of Doom," the hermit said. "We were looking for Seetha's gold!"

"Seetha?" Wiglaf cried. "The dragon?"

"No, Seetha the chipmunk!" The hermit glared at Wiglaf. "Yes, Seetha the dragon. Now, seven men followed me in. But I alone came out alive. Alive, yes. But nutty as a fruit-cake. That's why they call me Crazy Looey!"

Wiglaf hoped Looey wasn't both crazy and dangerous. He felt for his lucky rag.

"Oh, we read Seetha's warning," Crazy Looey went on. "But still I led my men deep into the cave. On the cave floor we saw a gold coin. I picked it up. And before you could say, 'The eensy, weensy spider went up the water spout...' " Crazy Looey started making little spider-climbing movements with his fingers.

"Go on, man!" Coach cried. "Go on!"

"Before you could say that," Crazy Looey said, "the cave filled with smoke. Poison smoke! I had set off a booby trap! My seven brave men dropped in their tracks. Dead as ducks. Deader, some of them. Me? I ran. Ran so fast, my hat fell off. It was my best hat, too. The one with a turkey feather—"

"Stop!" Erica called out. "I don't believe a word of this silly story!"

Wiglaf wasn't so sure. True, there was no Cave of Doom on Coach's map. But it sounded like a place Seetha would hide her gold.

"A red-and-white striped turkey feather," Crazy Looey went on. "The prettiest darn feather you ever did see."

"Enough, Cuckoo Looey!" Coach Plungett cried. "Let us pass!"

"That's *Crazy* Looey," the hermit said. "And

I won't let you pass! No way. Not a chance. Never!"

Coach Plungett drew his sword.

"Ah ha!" said Crazy Looey as the tip of Coach's sword touched the tip of his nose. "I see your point!"

The hermit did a little dance. Then he ran away down Snakes' Path, singing: "Down came the rain and washed the spider out...."

The Bloodhounds watched until he disappeared.

Coach put away his sword. "Shame on you for hiding, Bloodhounds!" he said. "You must face danger! Be manly men, like me!"

"Coach?" said Angus. "I don't want to die in the Cave of Doom! I want to go home to DSA! We could make it by sundown."

"Angus, you know Bloodhounds never turn back," Coach scolded. "Now, let's march!"

Wiglaf picked up his pack and started marching. He thought about what Crazy

Looey had said. He didn't mind poking about in caves with old mead flasks. Or even bears, so long as they were asleep. But the Cave of Doom sounded like a very different sort of cave. Wiglaf hoped Crazy Looey had made the whole thing up.

On they marched down Snakes' Path. They passed a large rock. It was shaped like a cow.

The Marley brothers began yelling, "Moo! Moo!"

Erica stopped marching. "Look!" she cried, pointing down at her feet.

Wiglaf looked. Spread across the path in front of him was a giant footprint.

"Is th-that a dragon print?" Angus asked.

"I think so," Erica said. "But we must be sure." She took *The Sir Lancelot Handbook* from her tool belt. She handed it to Wiglaf. "Read me Chapter Two: Are You Sure It's a Dragon Print?"

Wiglaf turned the tiny pages of the book.

At last he found the spot.

"*Dragon prints are big,*" he read. "*Very big.*"

Erica dropped to her knees. She looked at the print through her magnifying glass.

"Yes!" she cried. "This print is very big."

"*A dragon foot has three large toes,*" Wiglaf read. "*So does a dragon print.*"

"One, two, three!" Erica counted. "Yes!"

"*At the tip of each toe will be a deep hole made by a dragon claw,*" he read.

Erica brought her magnifying glass to the tip of the first toe. "Yes!" she cried. She jumped to her feet. "This is a dragon print!"

"Let's get out of here!" Angus howled.

Had this print been made by Seetha? Wiglaf wondered.

Erica called, "Coach! Come here! Quick!"

Coach Plungett hurried back to the spot.

"Egad!" he said when he saw the footprint.

"It's definitely a dragon print, sir," Erica told him.

"And look!" Wiglaf cried. He pointed to the side of the path. "There's another print! And another! They lead into the forest!"

"Put your noses to the ground, Bloodhounds!" cried Coach Plungett. "We shall follow these prints. For as sure as I'm a manly man, they were made by Seetha. And surely they shall lead us to her gold!"

Coach Plungett followed the giant footprints through the Dark Forest. The Bloodhounds followed Coach Plungett.

Wiglaf tried to keep up. But it wasn't easy. Branches scratched his face. Thorns tore at his britches. He had too many blisters to count. And the Marleys were burping again.

Angus turned around. "Here," he said. He handed Wiglaf a stick of his Wild Boar jerky. "This always makes me feel better."

"Thanks," Wiglaf said. But it did not make him feel better. It only made him thirsty.

On the Bloodhounds marched. At last the

dragon prints led to a creek. It was wide and deep. It smelled of dead fish. Thick green ooze lay on top of the water like a blanket. It reminded Wiglaf of something. But he could not think what.

"This is either Clear Water Creek," Coach said. "Or—" he turned the map sideways, "Stinking Green Creek."

Wiglaf had a pretty good idea which creek this was. And now he knew what it reminded him of—his mother's cabbage soup!

Erica took the spyglass from her tool belt. She held it to her eye. "I see dragon prints on the far side of the creek," she told Coach.

"Then we must wade across it," Coach said.

"No!" Angus cried. "Not across *that!*"

The Marleys began to grumble.

"There is no bridge," Coach pointed out. "Wading is the only way. Stop being such babies," he added. "What's a little stinking green ooze to manly men? Now follow me!"

"Sir?" Erica said. "There is another way." Erica took the rope from her tool belt. She threw one end over a tree branch that hung above the creek. Next, she made a loop. She pulled it tight around the branch. Then she knotted the end of the rope.

"Tah dah!" Erica cried. "We can swing across!"

Wiglaf grinned. Back home, he had swung across Pinwick Creek hundreds of times.

"I'll go first," Erica said. She backed up. Her tool belt jangled as she ran for the rope. She jumped on the knot. She swung easily across the creek and hopped off on the far bank.

"Well done!" cried Coach Plungett.

Erica beamed. "Who's next?" she called. She threw the rope over to the other side. Coach caught it. He swung across.

Charlie Marley went next. Then Barley. Then Farley. Harley burped as he swung over.

Harley threw Angus the rope. "Alas, Wiglaf!" Angus whispered. "I'm scared!"

"You can do it," Wiglaf said.

Angus made a few false starts. Then he stood on the knot. Wiglaf pulled the rope back. He gave Angus a mighty push.

Angus sailed over the creek. He landed on the far bank. "Easy as pie!" he exclaimed.

Angus threw Wiglaf the rope. Wiglaf caught it. He backed up. He began to run. He jumped and swung out over the creek.

It was just like swinging over Pinwick Creek—except for one thing. Back home, he never had a great big heavy pack on his back.

Wiglaf felt his fingers slip down the rope.

He lost his hold!

The next thing Wiglaf knew, he was falling toward the slimy green water.

Chapter 4

"Ayiiiiiiiiiiiiiiiiii!" Wiglaf screamed. He splashed down into Stinking Green Creek.

Stinking was right! The water smelled *exactly* like his mother's cabbage soup. Slimy green ooze trickled into Wiglaf's eyes. And his ears. And his mouth. Yuck!

On the bank, the Marleys roared with laughter.

"Wiggie!" Erica called. "Are you all right?"

"Don't swallow!" Angus yelled. "That water will kill you!"

Wiglaf spit out as much ooze as he could.

Coach held out a long tree branch. Wiglaf

took hold of it. He struggled toward the shore. At last he waded out of the water. He was stinking, green, and oozy.

The Marleys were laughing their heads off.

"Cut it out!" Erica growled at them. "It's not funny." She looked at Wiglaf. She put a hand to her mouth to keep from laughing. "Well, maybe it is. A little."

Angus couldn't help smiling, too.

Great, Wiglaf thought. *Now even my friends are laughing at me!* How he wished this class trip was over.

Wiglaf untied his lucky rag from his sword. He wrung it out. With it he wiped the green slime from his face and arms. He dried his hair. He patted off his clothes.

Coach slapped Wiglaf on the back. "Up and at 'em, now. That's the way. Are you ready to hit the road like a manly man?"

Wiglaf nodded. "Ready," he said. He was

sticky and wet. But he wasn't a quitter. He still wanted to find Seetha's gold.

"Take the lead, Eric," Coach said.

Erica grinned. "Let's march!" she called.

The Bloodhounds marched. They followed the prints onto a road. It was the very road Wiglaf had taken from his home in Pinwick to DSA. Soon the prints led back into the forest again. The afternoon sun dipped low in the sky. And still they followed the dragon prints.

Suddenly Erica stopped. "Coach!" she cried.

"Keep going, Eric," Coach said. "I see more prints over there."

"But we have seen them before!" Erica said. "We are back on Snakes' Path! See? The prints led us in a circle!"

"No jokes!" Angus cried. "I beg of you!"

"Upon my honor, I am not joking," Erica said. "Over there is the rock that looks like a cow. And here is the first print we found!"

Wiglaf saw that Erica was right. "Oh, flea bites!" he cried.

"Alas and alack!" Angus said sadly.

Only the Marleys didn't care. They'd found an anthill and were poking it with sticks.

"How did we *do* that?" Coach said. He took out the map again. He turned it this way and that. Then he pushed back his wig and scratched his hairless head for a long time.

Wiglaf staggered over to the cow-shaped rock. He leaned against it. He felt like crying. He was cold. His feet hurt. He smelled like dead fish. And all for nothing!

Wiglaf slid down against the rock. Then he noticed strange scratch marks on it. He squinted at the rock in the fading light. And he saw that the scratch marks were letters!

"Coach!" Wiglaf cried. "Over here! Hurry!"

Coach Plungett and the other Bloodhounds ran over. Erica lit her mini-torch. Scratched onto the rock by a dragon's claw was:

YOU FOLLOWED MY PRINTS
AND NOW—SURPRISE!
ALL YOU GOT WAS EXERCISE!
YOU'LL NEVER TRACK DOWN
MY HIDING SPOT!
FOR DRAGONS CAN FLY—
AND YOU CANNOT!
S E E T H A v o n F L A M B É
P.S. TURN BACK NOW!

"I say we take Seetha's advice!" Angus cried. "Let's turn back *now!*"

"Never!" Erica growled. "Seetha planned to lead us on this wild goose chase before she died. But her mean trick only makes me want to find her gold all the more!"

Wiglaf kicked at the cow-shaped rock. How he wished the Bloodhounds could turn back—just this once.

But Coach had other ideas.

"We shall camp here," he said. "The ground is hard and rocky. But manly men can sleep anywhere!"

The Bloodhounds got out their sleeping bags. Coach began setting up his tent.

In a low voice, Harley Marley called out, "Coach?"

Wiglaf stared. He had heard the Marleys burp. He had heard them laugh and whoop and moo like cows. But this was the first time he had heard any of them speak.

"Yes?" Coach answered. "What is it?"

"We'll set up your tent for you," Harley said. The other Marleys nodded.

Harley and Farley unfolded Coach's tent. Charlie and Barley pounded the tent poles into the ground. Wiglaf and Angus watched, wide-eyed.

At last camp was set up. The Bloodhounds made a fire. Coach passed out sandwiches.

"What *is* this?" Angus asked when he got his. "Hard bread and moldy cheese?"

Coach took a look. "No, you got the *moldy* bread and *hard* cheese sandwich."

Wiglaf pulled his wet sleeping bag close to the fire. He hoped it would dry. Then he stuck his sandwich on a stick. He toasted it over the campfire. It didn't make it taste any better. But at least it was warm going down.

Erica poured cider into her collapsible goblet. The rest of the Bloodhounds took turns drinking from the jug. Wiglaf hoped it was not the jug that had been home to Sir Mort's false teeth.

"Into your sleeping bags, Bloodhounds," Coach said after supper. "I am going to tell you a ghost story."

Wiglaf slid into his sleeping bag. It still smelled of fish. But it was almost dry.

"Once there lived an executioner," Coach began. "Every night at twelve o'clock, he took his axe and chopped off someone's head. He always wore a black hood. So no one knew what he looked like."

"Coach!" cried Angus. "This is too scary!"

"Oh, stop up your ears, Angus," Erica snapped. "The rest of us want to hear this."

Wiglaf wasn't so sure. A story about beheading was likely to be bloody. And Wiglaf's stomach turned over if he even thought about blood.

"The executioner," Coach continued, "walked through the Dark Forest with his axe. And as he went, he sang this song:

"If ever you hear me walking by,
*It may be **you** who's the next to die!*
I'll lay your neck on a chopping block,
And whack off your head at twelve o'clock!
I'll wrap you up in a big white sheet,
And bury you down six feet deep!
Then the worms crawl in! And the worms crawl out!

They'll eat your guts and then spit them out!
They'll peel your skin! They'll drink your blood!
Till all that's left are your bones in the mud!"

Wiglaf was about to stick his fingers in his ears. He didn't want to hear another word! But Coach went on with his tale. "The executioner chopped off hundreds and hundreds of heads. And then one day, it happened."

"What happened?" asked Erica.

"The executioner swung his axe too hard," Coach said. "And he chopped off his own bloody head!"

Uck! Wiglaf hoped he wouldn't be sick!

"The executioner's head rolled down a hill," Coach went on. "It splashed into Bottomless Lake and sank to the bottom."

"I'm glad he's dead!" Angus cried.

"Oh, he's dead, all right," Coach said. "But now his ghost walks through the Dark Forest.

He's looking for heads to chop off. For, you see, he needs a new head."

Angus began whimpering with fear.

Wiglaf held tight to his lucky rag.

"Now every night at midnight," Coach went on, "the ghost sings his song. So be careful in the Dark Forest, boys. If you hear someone singing: 'The worms crawl in, the worms crawl out...' Beware! It's the headless executioner, coming after *you!*"

Chapter 5

"**I**'m afraid to sleep," Angus whispered.

"Scaredy-cat!" Erica laughed. But Wiglaf thought that even her voice sounded shaky.

"Maybe it's not *this* Dark Forest," Angus said. "Maybe it's some *other* Dark Forest."

"Maybe," Wiglaf said. But as far as he knew there was only one Dark Forest.

Wiglaf heard a hissing sound. And another! He sat up in his sleeping bag. His heart was pounding. But it was only the Marleys. They were taking turns spitting into the campfire.

"Coach, I can't go to sleep," Angus said. "I'm afraid the ghost will come."

"Piffle!" Coach said. "I told you that story to make you brave. I want you to grow up to be a big, strong, manly man—like me!" He stood up. "I am going to my tent," he said. "Sleep well!"

"Good night, Coach!" Erica called.

"Sweet dreams!" called Harley Marley.

Then all the Marleys started laughing.

What is their problem? Wiglaf wondered.

Coach ducked into his tent. He closed the tent flap behind him. Wiglaf heard him humming a marching song as he got ready for bed.

Wiglaf closed his eyes. He heard owls calling. He heard crickets singing. He heard a Marley hocking something up from deep in his throat. He heard a horrible, bloodcurdling scream. Wiglaf's eyes popped open.

Suddenly Coach shot out of his tent. He held his sleeping bag tightly around him. He jumped around, screaming.

"The executioner's after him!" Angus cried. He disappeared into his sleeping bag.

"Help!" Coach screamed. "Don't let them get me!"

The Marleys rolled on the ground, laughing.

Coach kept jumping around. Then—*BONK!* He hit his head on a low tree branch. His nightcap and his wig stuck on the branch. But the rest of him fell to the ground.

Wiglaf jumped up. He forgot his own fear as he ran to his fallen leader.

"Coach?" Wiglaf cried. "Can you hear me?"

Coach didn't answer. He was out cold.

Erica reached Coach next. She patted his face. "Wake up, Coach!" she said.

The Marleys kept laughing and snorting.

At last Angus crawled out of his sleeping bag. He made his way slowly over to Coach. He poked him with his toe.

But Coach didn't move. Not even when

Wiglaf put his wig back on his head.

"What could have undone him so?" Erica asked. As if in answer, a sound came from inside Coach's tent: *Ribbit! Ribbit!*

Wiglaf and the others saw a dozen little frogs hop out of the tent. *Ribbit!* they croaked as they hopped away.

The Marleys laughed even harder.

Suddenly Wiglaf understood. No wonder the Marleys had been so helpful. They had planted the frogs inside Coach's tent!

"For a manly man," Angus said, "Coach sure is scared of frogs."

Erica splashed Coach with cold water from her canteen. At last Coach opened his eyes. He sat up. He smiled a strange smile.

"Hallo!" he said. "And who are you, young lads?"

"The Bloodhounds," Erica answered.

"You don't look like doggies!" Coach giggled.

"Uh-oh," said Angus.

"Coach?" Erica said. "Do you know your name?"

The silly smile appeared on Coach's face once more. "Is it...Rumpelstiltskin?"

"Guess again," Erica said.

"I know!" Coach exclaimed. "I'm Queen Mary!"

"He needs help," Erica said. "But nothing on my tool belt is going to do the trick."

"We have to get him to DSA," Wiglaf said.

"I'll take him!" Angus cried. He jumped up. "I'll do anything to get out of this forest!"

But Harley spoke up. "We'll take him," he said. His brothers nodded.

Wiglaf didn't think this was a very good idea. But he was not about to argue with the four big brothers.

Barley and Charlie held onto each other's arms, making a seat. Coach wobbled over and sat down on it. The Marleys lifted him up.

And they started off for DSA.

"Farewell from the queen!" Coach called. He blew kisses. Then he began to sing. "Queen Mary had a little lamb! Little lamb! Little lamb! Queen Mary had a little lamb! Its fleece was white as cheese!"

"All right, Bloodhounds!" Erica said to the two who were left. "It's just us now. We must find Seetha's gold for good old Coach Plungett! We shall make him proud of us. Because who is the best?"

"Who?" asked Angus.

"The Bloodhounds!" Erica cried.

The three of them pulled their sleeping bags into Coach's tent. They lined them up close together and crawled inside.

Wiglaf untied his lucky rag from his sword. He held it tightly and closed his eyes. He tried counting unicorns. After some two hundred, he finally fell asleep.

In the middle of the night, Wiglaf sat up

with a start. What had woken him? He listened. He heard a strange high voice, singing.

The little hairs on the back of Wiglaf's neck stood up. He squeezed his lucky rag. *Don't let it be the executioner's ghost!* he said over and over to himself.

The singing grew louder. The singer was coming closer!

"Does anybody hear singing?" Wiglaf whispered.

"Singing huh?" Angus said, waking up.

"I hear it," Erica said. She sounded scared.

The voice grew louder still.

Now they all heard what it was singing: *"Then the worms crawl in! And the worms crawl out! They'll eat your guts and then spit them out!"*

Angus gasped. "It's the executioner!"

Wiglaf slid out of his sleeping bag. He tiptoed over to the tent flap. He peeked outside. He didn't see a thing. But he heard the high voice more clearly now: *"They'll peel your skin!*

They'll drink your blood! Till all that's left are your bones in the mud!"

Erica began rattling the tools on her belt. "There must be something here I can use to make a ghost go away," she whispered.

Angus crawled over to Wiglaf. He, too, peeked out of the tent.

"There it is!" he whispered. He pointed with a shaky hand.

Wiglaf saw a shadowy shape.

"That can't be the executioner's ghost," Wiglaf told Angus. "It's too short."

"You'd be short, too, if you didn't have a head," Erica pointed out. "Call to it, Wiggie. Speak bravely. Maybe it won't harm us."

"Who...who...who goes there?" he said at last.

"Me!" called the shape.

"Me who?" Wiglaf called back.

"Me, Dudwin!"

Wiglaf gasped. He stuck his head out of the tent. "Dudwin?" he exclaimed. "Dudwin of Pinwick?"

"That's the one," the voice replied.

"Who is it, Wiglaf?" asked Erica. "What's going on?"

"Has he come to chop off our heads?" Angus whispered.

"It's not the ghost," Wiglaf said. "It's my little brother, Dudwin!"

Chapter 6

Wiglaf dashed out of the tent. He ran until he reached a sturdy boy of seven.

"Dudwin! It *is* you!" Wiglaf exclaimed. He saw that Dudwin had grown. And now—alas! His little brother was taller than he was!

Erica lit her mini-torch. She shone it on Wiglaf's brother. The boy had a round face and thick yellow hair. His tunic fit snugly over his belly. He wore baggy brown britches.

"Hallo, Wiggie!" Dudwin grinned. One front tooth was missing. He opened his arms and hugged Wiglaf—hard.

"Dudwin!" Wiglaf cried. "Let go!"

Dudwin did. "You smell like fish, Wiggie."

"What are you doing here, Dud?" Wiglaf asked, quickly changing the subject.

"I was on my way to your school," Dudwin explained. "Father sent me. He wants me to bring him all the gold you've got so far."

"Oh, great!" Wiglaf said under his breath.

"Dudwin," said Erica. "Why were you singing that worm song?"

"I like that song," Dudwin said. "Another one I like is 'Greasy, Grimy Gopher Guts.' Oh, and speaking of greasy..." Dudwin took a large flask from his pack. "Mother sent you some of her cabbage soup."

"Egad!" Wiglaf exclaimed. "I hoped never to taste that soup again as long as I live!"

"I love cabbage soup!" Angus cried. "If you don't want it, I'll take it!" He grabbed the flask from Dudwin. He popped the cork. He took a sniff. "Eeeeeew!" he cried. "Wiglaf! Is your own mother trying to poison you?"

"Sometimes I wonder," Wiglaf said. "But it

was kind of her to send it." He took the flask, put the cork back in place, and handed it to his brother. "Hold onto it for me, Dud."

They walked back to camp. The sun was coming up, so there was no use trying to sleep now. Erica rubbed two dry sticks together and lit a fire. They all sat around it, warming their cold hands. Wiglaf wished that he did not have to give his brother bad news.

"Dudwin," he said at last, "you must go home empty-handed. I have no gold yet."

Dudwin frowned. "Father won't like that."

"No. But he will like this," Wiglaf said. "Tell him that *I* am a dragon slayer!"

"Oh, right!" Dudwin laughed loudly. He slapped Wiglaf on the back—hard. "Tell me another one, Wiggie!"

"Two dragons have died by my hand," Wiglaf said. "Well, more or less, by my hand."

"Aw, go on!" Dudwin shot back.

"It's true," Angus put in.

"For real?" Dudwin asked Erica.

Erica nodded. "I helped him, of course."

"But Wiggie hates the sight of blood," Dudwin said. "Back home, he wouldn't even swat a fly. Once he cut his thumb and fainted. He never—"

"Never mind!" Wiglaf cut in. "You must go home after breakfast, Dudwin. Tell Father that when I have gold, I shall bring it myself."

"But Father thinks I'll be gone for a week," Dudwin said. "I don't want to go home yet!"

"You must," Wiglaf said. "We are hunting dragon treasure. You would be in the way."

"No, I wouldn't!" Dudwin cried. "I can help you! I'm good at finding treasure. I found lots on my way here." He emptied his pockets. "Look!" he said. "I found a diamond!"

"That's a sparkly rock, Dudwin," Wiglaf said.

Dudwin ignored his brother. "Here is a spur from the boot of a knight!" he went on.

"That's nothing but a piece of a pinecone!" Wiglaf said.

"And here is the best treasure of all," the boy said happily. "The tip of a wizard's wand!"

"That, Dudwin," Wiglaf growled, "is a twig!"

"Lighten up, Wiglaf," Erica said with a laugh. "Dudwin has some fine treasures."

Dudwin grinned. "Yeah. Lighten up, Wiggie."

Wiglaf rolled his eyes.

"Let him stay, Wiglaf," Angus added. "Dudwin can be an honorary Bloodhound."

"Oh, boy!" Dudwin cried.

"We shall soon find Seetha's gold," Erica pointed out. "And Dudwin can take some straight home to your father."

"Yes, yes!" Dudwin cried.

"Four is better than three," Angus said. "Dudwin can help us carry our gear."

This last point won Wiglaf over. "All right, Dudwin," he told his brother. "You can stay."

Dudwin grinned. "I was going to anyway, Wiggie," he said.

After breakfast, Erica called, "Blood-hounds, march!"

"Wait!" Dudwin cried. "I see a goblin's hat!" He ran off and picked up an acorn cap.

Erica tapped her foot and waited for him to come back. Then off they went.

Wiglaf marched behind Dudwin. Deep down, he felt glad that his brother was with them. True, Dudwin could be a pain. But he had his good points. After all, he was carrying a heavy pack. And this meant Wiglaf's own pack was lighter.

That morning, the Bloodhounds hunted for Seetha's treasure in Bats-a-Plenty Cave. They searched Chock-Full-of-Spiders Cave. And Leeches-R-Us Cave. They looked for treasure in cave after cave. But they came out of each one empty-handed.

Except for Dudwin.

"Oh, boy!" he cried, sliding out of Slippery Cave. "I found a baby dragon's tooth!"

"That's a pebble, Dud," Wiglaf said.

"Here is a fine treasure!" Dudwin called inside Slimy Cave. "A goblet fit for a king!"

"Dudwin!" Erica cried. "You took that from my tool belt!" She grabbed her goblet back.

Erica marched the Bloodhounds from cave to cave. The day grew hot. The Bloodhounds began to sweat. Mosquitoes bit them.

As they started over the Shiver River Bridge, Angus called, "Let's stop for a swim!"

"Bloodhounds never stop!" Erica said.

But halfway across the bridge, Erica stopped. And Wiglaf saw why.

A great hairy arm, waving a big spiked club, was sticking up from under the bridge.

"Yikes!" Angus cried. "It's a troll!"

"Right!" the troll roared. He pulled himself up onto the bridge. "And this is my bridge!"

The troll's eyes darted from face to face. "Who wants me to eat them first?" he roared.

No Bloodhound volunteered. Not even Erica.

"Someone step forward!" cried the troll. "If I eat you all at once, I'll get a bellyache!"

No Bloodhound stepped forward.

"You are one ugly troll!" Dudwin shouted.

"Shush, Dudwin!" Wiglaf clapped a hand over his brother's mouth.

Erica drew her sword. "Back off, troll!"

"Make me!" the troll cried. He swung his club and knocked Erica's sword into the river.

"Alas!" Erica cried. "That was my special Sir Lancelot look-alike sword!"

The troll laughed. He reached out a long arm, snatched up Angus, and dangled him over his mouth.

"No! Don't eat me!" Angus cried. "I'll give you a *bad* bellyache!"

"Hey, Troll-breath!" Dudwin yelled.

"Dudwin, stop it!" Wiglaf cried.

Dudwin paid no attention. "I have something much yummier than him!" he shouted.

"What?" the troll growled.

"Cabbage soup," Dudwin answered.

The troll eyed Dudwin. "Homemade?" he asked.

Dudwin nodded. "By my own mother."

"Give it here," said the troll.

Dudwin pulled the flask from his pack.

"Don't, Dudwin!" Wiglaf begged. "Mother's soup will make him *really* mad!"

But Dudwin stepped bravely up to the troll. He popped the cork off the flask. A sickening smell filled the air. Dudwin quickly splashed the soup in the troll's face.

The troll's eyes grew wide with surprise. He stuck out his tongue and licked some of the soup from his face. "Mmmmmmm!" he growled.

Wiglaf gasped. "You like it?" he cried.

"Like it?" said the troll. "I love it!" He dropped Angus onto the bridge. "I'll eat you humans later. Now, I want more soup!"

"You got it!" Dudwin said. He threw the flask to the troll.

While the troll gulped down the soup, the Bloodhounds ran across his bridge. They kept running until the troll was far behind. Then they fell down, gasping for breath.

"Nice work, Dudwin!" Erica exclaimed.

"*Very* nice," Angus said. "How is it that you were brave enough to stand up to the troll?"

"Oh, all my brothers are much meaner than the troll," Dudwin said. "Except for Wiglaf."

Wiglaf patted his brother on the back. He was proud of Dudwin. But at the same time, he felt—well, ashamed. His little brother was taller than he was. His little brother carried a bigger pack. And now his little brother had saved them from the troll. It was hard to take.

While Angus rested after his near-death-by-troll experience, Dudwin ran off. He was gone for a long time. Wiglaf was starting to worry when he came running back.

"Eric!" Dudwin cried. "Look what I found!"

"Shhh," Erica said. "I'm checking the map."

Dudwin ran over to Angus. "Look at this!" he exclaimed.

"Don't bother me, Dudwin," Angus said. "Not after what I've been through."

Dudwin turned to his brother. "Wiggie?"

Wiglaf sighed. "What did you find, Dud?"

Dudwin held out his hand to Wiglaf.

"Egad!" cried Wiglaf.

For there in Dudwin's grubby hand lay two golden coins.

Chapter 7

"Gold coins!" Wiglaf cried. "Where did you find them, Dudwin?"

"Gold?" Erica exclaimed. "Did you say *gold*?" She and Angus hurried over.

"I found them—" Dudwin began eagerly. Then he stopped. A strange look came over his face. "I'm not telling," he said.

"What?" Erica cried. "Why not?"

"Because," Dudwin said, "you keep making fun of my treasure."

"Don't be that way, Dudwin," Erica said. "Seetha must have dropped the coins on her way to her secret hiding place. Show us where you found them. The Cave of Doom will be close by. Come on, Dudwin!"

But Dudwin only shook his head *no*.

Erica pulled Wiglaf and Angus aside. "He's *your* brother, Wiglaf," Erica said in a low voice so Dudwin couldn't hear. "Make him tell!"

Wiglaf rolled his eyes. "What do you want me to do? Torture him?"

"If that's what it takes," Erica shot back.

Wiglaf really wanted to find the gold. If he did, he wouldn't have to send Dudwin home empty-handed. And he was sure Mordred would stop picking on him. He had to get Dudwin to tell where he found the coins so they could find the cave. He thought hard.

"Dudwin is stubborn," he told Erica at last. "Talking to him will do no good. But try offering him something from your tool belt."

Erica gasped. "I saved up for six months to buy this tool belt! Why should I be the one to bribe Dudwin?"

"Because you are the only one with any-thing to trade," Angus pointed out.

They walked back over to Dudwin.

"Dudwin," Erica said, "show us where you found the coins. If you do, I shall give you a tool from my Sir Lancelot Tool Belt."

"Oh, boy!" Dudwin cried. "Which one?"

"Well..." Erica said. "The toothpick."

Dudwin shook his head.

"The lice comb?"

"No way," Dudwin said.

Erica sighed. "What do you want?"

Dudwin grinned. "The torch."

"What?" Erica cried. "That is my best tool!"

Dudwin jingled the coins in his pocket.

Erica took the torch from her belt. She looked at it longingly. Then she handed it to Dudwin.

"Oh, boy!" Dudwin exclaimed. "Now I can find treasures in the dark!"

"Cut the chitchat," Erica snapped. "Show us where you found the coins."

Dudwin led the way through the forest. He stopped at the foot of a big hill, covered with vines. "There," he said.

"Clear the brush, Bloodhounds!" Erica ordered. "Keep a lookout for coins!"

Wiglaf and Angus drew their swords. They began hacking away at the vines. But they found that the vines were not really growing on the hill. They had only been piled up there as if to hide something. The boys pulled the vines away and discovered a great hole in the side of the hill.

"It's the mouth of a cave!" cried Angus.

Wiglaf's eyes grew wide. Pointed rocks hung down over the cave entrance. It looked exactly like the open mouth of a dragon!

A wooden sign had fallen face down beside the entrance. Wiglaf picked it up. It said:

WELCOME TO
THE CAVE OF DOOM!

Wiglaf quickly dropped the sign. They had found the Cave of Doom!

"Footprints!" Erica cried suddenly. "Going into the cave!" She studied the prints with her magnifying glass. "They're Seetha's, all right," she said. "I'm going in. Who's going with me?"

"Not me," said Angus.

"Me!" cried Dudwin.

"No, Dud," Wiglaf said. "You stay out here with Angus. I—I'll go in."

"But it's dark in the cave." Dudwin held up the torch. "And I have the light."

"Good point," Erica said. "And very brave of you to want to come." She shot Angus a look.

"Oh, all right," Angus said. "I'll come, too."

"All right, Bloodhounds," Erica said. "Let's go in!"

"Not so fast!" called a voice behind them. "Not so fast!"

Wiglaf whirled around. There, sitting on his throne-like chair, was Mordred!

"Greetings, Bloodhounds!" Mordred smiled at them. None of the skinny student teachers were smiling. They were struggling to put their heavy headmaster down gently.

"I have come to see how you are doing," Mordred said. "Where is Plungett?"

"He had an accident, Uncle," Angus said. "The Marley brothers took him back to DSA."

"Egad!" Mordred cried. "I hope he is not hurt badly. It would not be easy to find a new slaying coach. Not at the salary I pay." His violet eyes lit upon Dudwin. "And who, pray tell, is *this?*"

"Dudwin," Wiglaf answered. "My brother."

"Why in the name of King Ken's britches is your big brother here?" Mordred barked.

"He's my *little* brother," Wiglaf said. "But, sir! We have found Seetha's hiding spot. Somewhere inside this cave is her gold."

Wiglaf had said the magic word: gold.

Mordred jumped down from his chair. "Oh, joy!" he cried. "Oh, happy day! Come! I shall lead you into the cave myself!"

Mordred took a step toward the dark mouth of the cave. Then he stopped.

"On second thought," he said, "I shall *follow* you Bloodhounds into the cave. That way I can make sure nothing sneaks up on you from behind." Mordred pointed at Dudwin. "You with the torch!" he said. "Lead the way!"

"To the treasure!" Dudwin yelled. And he ran into the cave.

Wiglaf, Erica, and Angus hurried after him. The torchlight threw tall shadows onto the stony walls. High above Wiglaf's head long, thin stalactites hung down from the ceiling. There were hundreds of them. They looked like stone fangs!

"Don't dawdle!" Mordred called from behind. "Do you see any sign of the gold?"

"Not yet, sir!" Erica called back.

Suddenly Dudwin tripped. The torch flew from his hand as he fell.

Wiglaf reached down to help him up. As he picked up the torch, he saw that his brother had fallen over a pile of white shapes. It took him a moment to understand what they were.

"B-b-b-bones!" Wiglaf cried.

"Bones?" Angus screamed. He took off for the mouth of the cave.

"Oof!" Mordred grunted as his nephew ran into him. He grabbed Angus's arm.

"Let go!" Angus cried. "I'm out of here!"

"Are you mad?" Mordred roared. "We're so close to Seetha's gold, I can almost smell it!"

"I think that smell is dried bat droppings, sir," Erica offered.

"Whatever," Mordred said. He turned Angus around. "Onward!"

"Whose bones are they, Wiggie?" Dudwin asked as they began inching forward.

"Some big animal probably died here long ago," Wiglaf said. He hoped it was true.

"I want to keep some," Dudwin said. He began picking up bones.

"What's the holdup?" Mordred yelled from the back of the line. "Go! Go! Go!"

"What's this?" Erica said. She bent down. But instead of a bone, she picked up a hat.

Wiglaf stared at the thing in Erica's hand. "What is stuck in that hat?" he asked.

"Looks like a red-and-white striped turkey feather," Erica answered. "And it is the prettiest darn feather I ever did see."

"This must be Crazy Looey's hat!" Wiglaf

cried. "And these bones! They must be the bones of his seven brave men!"

"Move!" Mordred called. "Moooove!"

"We are doomed!" Angus howled.

"I'm too young to get doomed!" Dudwin cried. The torchlight wavered as his hand began to shake. "I want to go back, Wiggie!"

"Be brave, Dudwin," Wiglaf whispered. "You are a Bloodhound now. And Bloodhounds never turn back. Besides," he added, "Mordred won't let you turn back."

Wiglaf untied his lucky rag from his sword.

"Here, Dudwin," he said, handing it to him. "This has always brought me luck. I am sure it will keep you from being doomed."

"Thanks, Wiggie." Dudwin sniffed. He held the rag tightly as he began walking again.

Erica started singing in a shaky voice: *"We're the mighty Bloodhounds...We're dogged and we're bold..."*

The others joined in. Their voices echoed as they walked toward a faint yellow glow far back in the cave. They followed Dudwin through a passageway. They came out in a big open space lit by a strange, yellow light.

Wiglaf blinked. And then he saw before him a life-sized statue of Seetha! Her wings were spread. Her tail was curled around a giant stone bowl. And piled high in the bowl were bright, shining golden coins!

Mordred pushed past Wiglaf. "Gold!" he cried. Tears of joy sprang to his eyes. "A mountain of gold! And it all belongs to ME!"

Chapter 8

"**D**on't start counting your gold yet, sir!" Wiglaf said. "Look! Seetha has left us a message on the wall!" And he began to read what had been scratched in stone:

If I die, I, Seetha von Flambé, leave all my gold to my 3,683 children. To anyone else who finds my gold—anyone who is NOT one of my beautiful children—I leave this warning:

GO AWAY! GO FAR AWAY!
DO NOT COME BACK SOME OTHER DAY!
FOR IF YOU STEAL A COIN—JUST ONE...
YOU'LL MEET YOUR DOOM—

IT WON'T BE FUN.
SMOKE WILL CHOKE YOU!
FIRES WILL BLAZE!
THE CAVE WILL SHAKE!
YOU'LL BE AMAZED!
SPEARS SHALL RAIN DOWN FROM ON HIGH!
AND <u>YOU</u> SHALL BE THE NEXT TO DIE!

"I'm scared!" Dudwin cried.

"Me, too!" Angus said.

Wiglaf started shaking.

Even Erica looked scared.

"Don't be such sausages!" Mordred cried. "What else would a dragon say? 'Go ahead. Help yourself to all my gold!' I don't think so!"

"Please Uncle Mordred!" Angus fell to his knees. "Let's get out of here! I beg you! Seetha may be dead. But she means business!"

"Fiddlesticks!" Mordred barked. "Stop stalling, all of you! Go get my gold!"

Then, to Wiglaf's horror, Dudwin spoke up. "You're the one who wants the gold," he told Mordred. "So why don't you get it yourself?"

"What?" roared Mordred. "Me? Don't you know why boys were invented? So grown-ups never have to do anything they don't want to! Now, *go get my gold!*"

The Bloodhounds stayed close together. They inched toward the bowl of treasure.

"Okay," said Erica when they reached it. "Who shall take the first coin from the pile?"

Wiglaf swallowed. Here was a chance for him to do a brave deed. Besides, if taking a coin set off a booby trap, what did it matter who took it? They were all goners.

"I'll do it," Wiglaf said. He drew a breath. Slowly he slid a coin from the pile. He waited for the smoke and fire.

But nothing happened.

Mordred cried, "What did I tell you, boys? Seetha's warning was pure poppycock!"

Then Wiglaf heard a low rumble.

"Is that your stomach?" he asked Erica.

"No," she said. "I thought it was yours."

The rumbling grew louder.

"Ohhh!" howled Angus. "It's doom time!"

Wiglaf swallowed. He quickly tossed the coin back onto the pile of gold.

Too late!

The rumbling thundered louder. Then the gold in the big stone bowl started to spin around and around. It quickly picked up speed. The coins circled the bowl faster and faster. Then, as if someone had pulled a plug at the bottom of the bowl, the coins began to disappear down a hole. *SLUUUUUURP!*

"What's happening?" Mordred cried.

"The gold is going down some kind of drain!" Angus answered.

"WHAT?" Mordred screamed. And he started running toward the stone dragon.

The Bloodhounds jumped out of the way as the headmaster took a flying leap into the bowl. He slid down, grabbing for the coins.

There was a final *SLURP!* Then it was still.

"All is not lost!" Mordred cried happily. "I have a great big handful of gold!"

Mordred tried to pull his arm out. But his fist, full of coins, was stuck in the hole.

"Help me, lads!" Mordred cried.

The Bloodhounds held onto Mordred's boots. They pulled with all their might. At last...*POP!* Off came the boots.

"You ninnies!" Mordred cried. "Pull *me!*"

The Bloodhounds grabbed Mordred's feet. They pulled as hard as they could. But his fist stayed stuck.

"Stop," Mordred cried at last. "Leave me here, boys. Carry on at DSA as best you can without me. It won't be easy. But you must try!"

"But Uncle Mor—" Angus began.

"No, nephew," Mordred said. "Do not try to comfort me. My death will be slow. Slow and very terrible. But I shall be brave and—"

"Sir?" Erica cut in.

"Quiet!" Mordred snapped. "As I was saying, I shall be brave. And so it is fitting that one of the DSA towers be named for me. The north one, I think. Mordred's Tower. That has a nice ring to it."

"You don't have to die here, sir!" Wiglaf said. "You *can* save yourself!"

"Blazing King Ken's britches!" Mordred cried. "Are you going to pester me to death? Well, tell me, boy. How can I save myself?"

And Wiglaf said, "Let go of the gold."

"Let go?" Mordred looked puzzled.

"Yes, Uncle!" Angus answered. "Then your hand can slide out of the hole."

Mordred frowned. "You cannot mean I should give up the gold? No. Never."

Wiglaf turned to Erica. "We have to get out of here!" he said. "What shall we do?"

"I don't know," Erica said. "But Sir Lancelot will." She yanked *The Sir Lancelot Handbook* from her belt. She began turning pages. "Ah ha!" she cried happily. "Here, under 'Emergencies.'" She began to read aloud: *"Emergency #54: Is there a great big greedy man whose hand is stuck down a hole because he won't let go of a fist full of gold coins?"*

"Yes!" cried Angus. "Yes! That's it exactly!"

"If the great big greedy man doesn't hurry up and let go," Erica read on, *"are you in danger of being doomed?"*

"Yes!" Angus cried. "Right again!"

Erica read on. *"When all else fails..."* She turned the page. *"...try tickling!"*

"Oh, boy!" Dudwin cried.

Then all four Bloodhounds jumped on Mordred.

"Stop!" cried Mordred. "What are you doing?"

"Sorry, sir," Erica said. She was tickling his belly. "But it's for your own good."

"Hoo-hoo!" Mordred howled. "Oh! Stop!"

No one stopped. Angus tickled Mordred's left foot. Wiglaf did the same to his right. Dudwin chucked him under the chin.

Mordred wiggled and giggled. He kicked and screamed, "Have mercy!"

But the Bloodhounds kept on. At last Wiglaf heard *Clink! Clink! Clink!* as the coins fell from Mordred's fist.

"It worked!" he cried.

"Of course it did!" Erica exclaimed. "Sir Lancelot has never let me down!"

"Noooo!" Mordred sobbed as his hand—his empty hand—popped out of the hole. He pushed away the ticklers. His eyes glowed with red-hot fury.

"Trick *me* out of my gold, will you?" he cried. He pulled on his boots. "Wait till I get my hands on you!"

"But, sir!" Erica said. "We couldn't leave you here to die!"

"Don't argue with him!" Wiglaf said. "Let's go!"

"Wait!" Dudwin yelled. "I spy treasure!"

"Treasure?" Mordred cried. "Where?"

Dudwin pushed the torch into Wiglaf's hand. Then he started climbing up the dragon statue.

"Stop!" Wiglaf cried. "Dudwin! Come back down!"

But Dudwin kept climbing. And now Wiglaf saw why. Between its stone teeth, the dragon statue held one last gold coin.

Mordred's eyes lit up as he saw it, too. He lunged for the statue.

"There is just one coin, boy!" the headmaster roared. "Just one! And it's mine!"

One coin. Just one. Seetha's warning rang inside Wiglaf's head.

FOR IF YOU STEAL A COIN—JUST ONE...
YOU'LL MEET YOUR DOOM—
IT WON'T BE FUN.

Now Wiglaf understood. Seetha's warning was about one coin—just one! And suddenly he knew that the warning wasn't poppycock at all.

"Don't touch that coin!" Wiglaf yelled to the climbers. "Don't touch it!"

Too late! Mordred had already snatched the coin from between the dragon's teeth.

"Ha ha!" he cried. "I got it first! I got—"

Mordred got no further.

A flame shot from the statue's mouth.

"Yowie!" Mordred cried. He jumped down.

Dudwin jumped down, too.

Smoke began to pour from the stone dragon's nose. More flames shot from between its jaws. The cave walls began to shake.

THWUNK! A stalactite dropped from the ceiling.

Wiglaf stared at the quivering stone spear in front of him. It had missed him by inches!

THWUNK! Another dropped beside him.

THWUNK! And another!

And then, just as Seetha had warned, hundreds of stone spears began raining down.

"Help!" cried Angus. "We're doomed!"

Chapter 9

Wiglaf grabbed Dudwin's hand. He ran through the smoke, pulling his brother with him.

THWUNK! A stalactite landed right behind them.

Wiglaf dropped the torch. It hit the cave floor and sputtered out. The cave was dark now. And filled with smoke. Wiglaf could hardly breathe. But he kept going. Far off, he thought he saw light. The mouth of the cave!

THWUNK!

Wiglaf jumped back from the stalactite. Dudwin's hand slid out of his.

THWUNK! THWUNK! THWUNK!

Stone spears were falling thick and fast! Wiglaf ran for his life. He thought his brother was ahead of him. "Run toward the light, Dudwin!" he yelled.

Wiglaf heard a *whoosh* as Mordred raced by him.

At last, Wiglaf reached the mouth of the cave. He ran out into the daylight, gasping for air.

He saw Erica. And Mordred was leaning against the student teachers, catching his breath. But where was Dudwin?

Wiglaf heard footsteps. That had to be his brother. But a second later, Angus ran out of the cave.

"I'm not doomed after all!" Angus cried.

Wiglaf ran back to the mouth of the cave. "Dudwin?" he called. "Are you in there?"

"I'm stuck!" came the faint reply. "Help me, Wiggie!"

"I'm coming!" Wiglaf raced back into the cave. Falling stalactites whistled by him.

"Over here, Wiggie!" the boy cried.

Wiglaf turned toward the voice. At last he found his brother. A stalactite had stabbed through Dudwin's baggy britches, pinning him to the spot.

Wiglaf tugged on the stalactite. He pulled with all his might. But it stayed stuck.

"Step out of your breeches, Dud," Wiglaf said. "Hurry! You'll have to leave them here."

"No way!" Dudwin cried. "My treasures are in my pockets."

Wiglaf groaned. He didn't have time to argue. He felt like giving his stubborn little brother a kick in the shin. Instead, he drew back his foot and kicked the stalactite—hard!

Snap! It broke off at the base.

"Oooh!" Wiglaf cried. Had he broken all his toes, too?

"Way to go, Wiggie!" cried Dudwin.

Wiglaf grabbed Dudwin again. He forgot about his throbbing toes as he pulled his brother toward the light.

Then, to his horror, he saw that stone spears were falling right inside the mouth of the cave. And falling fast! The entrance was almost blocked!

"Faster, Dud!" Wiglaf cried. "Faster!" Wiglaf pushed Dudwin—hard! His brother half flew out of the cave.

Wiglaf dove after him. He rolled away as the spears filled the mouth of the cave. He lay on the ground, panting.

Dudwin raced over to Wiglaf. He helped him up. He threw his arms around him.

"Wiglaf!" he cried. "You saved my life!"

"Pipe down, you blasted boys!" Mordred yelled. "If not for you, I'd be a rich man!"

"A rich *dead* man," Angus added.

Dudwin ran over to Mordred. "I want to be

like my brave big brother! I want to go to Dragon Slayers' Academy. Can I? Please?"

"You must be joking!" Mordred cried. "Wiglaf still owes me his seven pennies. You think I would let his brother in for free?"

"I can pay!" Dudwin said. He reached into his pocket. He pulled out his two gold coins.

Mordred's eyes almost popped out of his head. "Those are *my* coins!" he roared. "I dropped them! Right in the spot where you found them!"

Dudwin pulled his hand back. "I'm not falling for *that* old trick!"

"Give him one coin, Dud," Wiglaf whispered. "Or you shall lose both of them."

"If you say so, Wiglaf," Dudwin said.

And he threw one coin in a bush.

Mordred dove after it.

"Now run home with the other coin," Wiglaf said. "Quickly, Dud! Before Mordred tries to get his hands on it!"

Dudwin slipped the coin into his pocket. He picked up his pack. He gave Wiglaf back his lucky rag. "It worked, Wiggie," Dudwin said. "I didn't get doomed."

"Farewell, Dudwin!" Wiglaf said.

"Goodbye, Wiggie!" Dudwin smiled. "I'll tell them at home how you saved my life in the Cave of Doom! I'll tell them you are a hero!"

Dudwin waved and took off for the road.

Mordred crawled out from under the bush. He held up the gold coin. "Got it!" he cried.

"Excuse me, sir?" Erica said.

"What now?" Mordred asked as he got to his feet.

"We Bloodhounds found Seetha's gold," Erica said. "So we should get the prize."

"Oh! You want a prize, do you?" Mordred showed all his teeth in a fierce grin. "And so you shall have one!"

Wiglaf didn't like the way Mordred said that.

"Student teachers!" Mordred called. "Take the rest of the day off."

"Oh, thank you, sir!" cried the thin ones.

Mordred stomped over to his throne-like chair. He sat down.

"Wiglaf, for your prize, take the right front pole!" he ordered. "Eric, left front! Angus, you take the two in the rear! Pick me up all at once, boys. No bouncing!"

Wiglaf struggled to pick up his part of the large headmaster. He groaned as he took a step.

"Faster, boys!" Mordred cried. "Or we shall never make it home by nightfall!"

"Things could be worse," Erica said bravely as they staggered toward DSA.

Wiglaf nodded. And once they got there, he thought, they probably would be. But for now

Wiglaf felt glad that he had sent his brother home with a gold coin. And with a true story about Wiglaf, the hero.

This time he started the singing:

"We're the mighty Bloodhounds!
We're dogged and we're bold!
We're the mighty Bloodhounds!
And we found Seetha's gold!"

DRAGON SLAYERS'
ACADEMY™ 4

A WEDDING
FOR WIGLAF?

KATE McMULLAN

Chapter 1

Wiglaf pushed his carrot-colored hair off his sweaty brow. It was a hot spring day. Coach Plungett had given his class a break to get a drink. Wiglaf and the other students stood in line at the well in the castle yard, waiting for a turn with the dipper.

Coach leaned against the well. "I've killed many a dragon, lads," he said. "Ah, yes...but I'll never forget the first. You never do. Hotblaze was his name. The beast spewed flames so hot they melted my helmet. Burned my hair off, too. Been bald as a potato ever since. But that didn't stop me. I drew my sword like a manly man! I jabbed Hotblaze in his left flank. Or...was it his right?" Coach pushed back his brown, pageboy-style wig. He scratched his hairless head, trying to think.

Wiglaf hoped Coach wouldn't go on and on, telling how Hotblaze met his end. Blood-and-guts stories always made him feel sick to his stomach.

"Wiglaf!" someone called.

Wiglaf turned. He saw his friend Angus hurrying across the castle yard.

"Uncle Mordred wants to see you in his office right away!" Angus yelled.

Me? Wiglaf pointed to himself.

"Go on, lad," Coach told Wiglaf. "You can get the homework from Torblad."

"Nice knowing you, Wiglaf," Torblad scoffed.

Wiglaf trotted off. He was glad to get out of class. But he hated to think why he was being summoned by the hot-tempered headmaster of Dragon Slayers' Academy.

Mordred was not fond of Wiglaf. For Wiglaf had, quite by accident, killed two dragons, Gorzil and Seetha. But he had not brought Mordred any of their dragon gold.

Wiglaf caught up with Angus. "What does Mordred want?" he asked. The two began hurrying toward the old castle that housed DSA.

Angus shrugged. "Uncle Mordred didn't say. But he wasn't angry. In fact, he seemed rather...jolly."

"Jolly?" Wiglaf exclaimed. That was a new one. Mordred was never jolly.

The boys ran all the way to Mordred's office. Angus knocked on the door.

"Enter!" boomed a voice.

The boys entered. They found Mordred standing next to his desk, reading a copy of

The Medieval Times. He wore a red velvet tunic with golden dragons stitched on it.

"Ah, Wiglaf!" Mordred put down his newspaper. "Back to work, Angus," he added, never taking his violet eyes from Wiglaf. "I don't pay you half a penny a year to stand around gawking!"

"No, Uncle," Angus said. He went back to polishing the headmaster's big black boots.

"Ah, Wiglaf!" Mordred exclaimed again. "How are you feeling, my boy? Fit as a fiddle, I hope?"

"Yes, thank you, sir," Wiglaf answered. He wondered why the headmaster had asked. Mordred was not one to worry about the health of his students. Quite the opposite, in fact.

"And your pet pig," Mordred went on. "Is Daisy happy living out in the henhouse?"

"Very happy, sir," Wiglaf answered.

It surprised him that Mordred knew about

Daisy. He had brought his dear pig to school with him from his home in Pinwick. He wondered if Mordred also knew that Daisy was under a wizard's spell. She could speak—in Pig Latin.

"Is Frypot feeding you enough lumpen pudding?" Mordred asked.

"More than enough, sir," Wiglaf said.

"Excuse me, Uncle Mordred," Angus said. He held up a boot. "Is this shiny enough for you?"

"You must be joking!" Mordred yelled. "Put some elbow grease into it, nephew!"

Angus sighed and went back to polishing.

"Now, about clothes, Wiglaf," Mordred said. "My sister Lobelia will order you a new tunic. And fine new britches, too."

"Clothes?" Wiglaf said. "But I have no money! I cannot pay for new clothes."

"Worry not, my boy," Mordred said, still smiling. "I shall pay for everything!"

Wiglaf gasped. Now he understood. Mordred had lost his mind!

The DSA headmaster was a famous penny-pincher. He never spent a cent if he could help it. He would never, in a million years, pay for anything for anybody else. Especially not for Wiglaf.

There was a sudden knock on the door.

"Enter!" Mordred said.

The door flew open. Erica ran into the office. Erica dressed as a boy so she could go to DSA. Everyone there called her Eric. Wiglaf was the only student who knew that she was a girl. And a royal one at that. She was none other than Princess Erica, daughter of Queen Barb and King Ken.

"Sir!" Erica cried. "Come quickly! Torblad fell into the moat. And he cannot swim!"

"Torblad, eh?" Mordred scratched his chin thoughtfully. "I wonder if he is all paid up.

Let me check my records." He opened a worn leather book. On the cover, it said:

MORDRED'S MONEY
Private! Keep Out! No Peeking! I Mean It!

"Hmmm. Just as I thought," the headmaster muttered. "Torblad owes me for two semesters." Mordred jumped up suddenly. "Egad!" he cried. "If he drowns, I'll never see a penny of it! Wait here, Wiglaf. I'll be back!" The headmaster raced from the room. Erica raced after him.

Wiglaf turned to Angus. "Your uncle has gone mad!" he said. "Why else would he offer to buy me new clothes?"

"Oh, he has something up his sleeve," Angus said. "You can be sure of that." He put down the boot he was polishing. He picked up Mordred's copy of *The Medieval Times*. "Let's see if Dragon Stabbers' Prep beat Knights-R-Us in the jousting match," he said.

"Wait," said Wiglaf. "What's this on the front page?" Together, the boys read the headline story.

BELCHEENA WORTH BILLIONS
Super-Rich Princess Seeks Husband
EAST ARMPITTSIA *Wednesday, June 8—*

Years ago, Princess Belcheena's heart was broken. The love of her life rode off, never to be seen again. The princess shut herself up in her tower in Mildew Palace. She comforted herself by counting her gold. She has great mountains of it, so counting it took a long time. But last week, she finished. Now the princess has come out into the world again. And she is looking for a husband.

"I have over twelve billion in gold coins," the princess told reporters on Monday. "Now all I need is a special someone to help me spend it. Princes seek wives all the time," she added. "Why shouldn't a princess seek a husband?"

There are three things the princess is looking for in her future groom. He must be a dragon slayer.

He must be a redhead. And his name must begin with Princess Belcheena's favorite letter of the alphabet—W.

"The matchmaker who finds me the right husband will get a pot of gold," the princess promised.

Angus whistled. "Belcheena is loaded!"

"I wonder why her true love rode away," Wiglaf said.

Just then the door swung open. Mordred was back. His hair and his tunic dripped with foul-smelling moat water.

"Torblad is saved," he growled. "But he had better pay up soon. Or I'll throw the little rotter back into the moat myself."

Mordred glanced at Angus and Wiglaf. "Ah, you've seen the paper!" he said. "I guess my little surprise is out of the bag. Eh, Wiglaf?"

"Your surprise, sir?" Wiglaf asked.

"Yes, my boy," Mordred said happily. "You are about to get married!"

Chapter 2

"Excuse me, sir?" Wiglaf managed. "I don't think I heard you right."

"You...are...about...to...get...married," Mordred said again.

Wiglaf looked over his shoulder. Mordred had to be speaking to someone behind him.

But there was no one behind him.

"You cannot mean Wiglaf," Angus said.

"Oh, but I do!" Mordred picked up the paper. "Belcheena says her husband must be a dragon slayer. And Wiglaf has slain two dragons."

"But only by accident, sir!" Wiglaf cried. "Surely the princess wants a husband who slew his dragons on purpose."

"Fiddle-faddle," Mordred said. He glanced at the paper again. "Belcheena wants a red-headed husband. And you, Wiglaf, are a red-head."

"My hair is orange, sir," Wiglaf pointed out.

"Close enough," Mordred growled. "Next you will tell me that Wiglaf does not begin with *W!*"

"No, sir," Wiglaf said miserably.

"Well then!" Mordred boomed. "It looks as if I shall be a matchmaker! And I shall get the pot of gold!" He rubbed his hands together. "Ha! I knew there was an easier way to get rich than sending half-witted boys out to bring me dragon gold!"

Mordred glanced at the sundial on his desk. "Off with you now, Wiglaf," he said. "Come back after supper tonight. Lobelia will be here then. And we'll make plans for your wedding!"

Wiglaf fell to his knees. "I am a peasant!" he

cried. "My twelve brothers smell bad, for my father thinks bathing causes madness! My—"

"Say no more, Wiglaf," Mordred cut him off. "I understand what you are telling me."

"Oh, do you, sir?" Wiglaf cried happily.

"Certainly," Mordred said. "You don't want to invite your family to the wedding."

"Uh...that is not exactly what I meant, sir," Wiglaf said. "I was trying to explain how very unfit I am to mar...mar..." He could not bring himself to say the awful word! "How unfit I am for a princess," he said at last.

Mordred frowned. "You are a redheaded dragon slayer named Wiglaf. You are exactly what the princess wants. I shall make this known to her. And I shall get the pot of gold. I wonder," he added dreamily, "just how big a pot it is?"

Mordred stared into space, imagining his pot of gold. The boys quietly left his office. They headed for Scrubbing Class.

"Can your uncle really make me get mar...
mar..." Try as he might, Wiglaf could not say
it! "Can he make me do this thing?" Wiglaf
asked.

"He seems to think so," Angus said.

They walked in silence for a while. Then
Angus said, "Do not take this the wrong way,
Wiglaf. But when the princess sees you,
surely she will put a stop to any wedding."

"I hope you're right," Wiglaf said. But he
was worried. Mordred was so set on getting
that pot of gold.

The boys reached the DSA kitchen. Frypot
stood at the door. "Hurry in to class, boys," he
called. "You may think Scrubbing is not as
exciting as Slaying Class. But wait until you
make a kill. It's a mess, what with the dragon
guts hanging off your sword and all. Then
you'll be glad you took old Frypot's Scrubbing
Class."

Wiglaf hurried over to Erica on the far side

of the room. She was scraping burned lumpen pudding from a big pot. *How like Erica to pick the dirtiest pot,* Wiglaf thought. No wonder she always won the Dragon Slayer of the Month medal.

"Wiglaf!" Erica cried when she saw him. "What were you doing in Mordred's office?"

"I'll tell you," Wiglaf whispered. "But first I must ask you something. Do you princesses—"

"Talk not of princesses!" Erica hissed. "If you have breathed a word of my secret, Wiglaf..."

"I have said nothing!" Wiglaf said. "I swear it on my sword!"

"Ha!" Erica scoffed. "That rusty old thing?"

"I shall never tell your secret," Wiglaf said. "But tell me! Do you know Belcheena?"

"Belcheena!" Erica cried.

Several heads turned toward them.

"Shhhh!" Wiglaf whispered. "What is she like?"

"Belcheena doesn't come out of her tower much," Erica said. "But I saw her once at a Princess Talent Contest. That was the day I won first prize in sword fighting! True, only one other princess had entered, but I—"

"What about Belcheena?" Wiglaf put in.

"As I remember, she sang a sad song. 'The Squire of My Desire,' I think. Why do you ask, Wiglaf?"

"There is a story about her in the paper," Wiglaf said. "She is looking for a husband."

"Belcheena is very..." Erica stopped for a moment. "How shall I put it? Belcheena has a very strong personality. I pity the man who marries her."

"Then you may have to pity me!" Wiglaf cried. And he told Erica all that had taken place in Mordred's office.

"I have no wish to marry *anyone*," Wiglaf finished up. "I want to stay here at DSA with my friends. I want to become a knight someday. I want to travel the kingdom, helping villagers. And saving small, helpless animals—"

"Yes, yes," Erica broke in. "So tell Mordred that you won't marry Belcheena."

"But she has promised a pot of gold to the matchmaker who finds her a redheaded, dragon-slaying, *W*-named husband," Wiglaf said. "And Mordred has his heart set on this pot."

"Ah," Erica said. "Mordred is after her gold, is he? Well then, if I were you, Wiggie, I know what I'd be doing right now."

"What?" Wiglaf cried. "Tell me!"

Erica smiled. "I'd be picking out the perfect spot for my honeymoon!"

Chapter 3

The lumpen pudding that night was even worse than usual. Frypot had burned it to a crisp. But he hacked the blackened glop to pieces and served it anyway.

After supper, Wiglaf felt sick. But he didn't know if it was from the pudding or the thought of getting mar...mar... Oh, he could not even think it! Slowly he made his way to Mordred's office.

Mordred beamed as he let Wiglaf in. "Here he is, Lobelia. The lucky groom!"

Lobelia smiled. She had violet eyes and thick dark hair like Mordred. But there the likeness between brother and sister ended.

Lobelia was thin and known for her high style.

"Sit, Wiglaf," Mordred said.

Wiglaf sat down across from Mordred's desk.

"I have written to Belcheena." Mordred handed Wiglaf a sheet of parchment. "This is a first draft. Read it—quickly! I shall have Brother Dave up in the—oh, what do you call that room in the tower with all the books?"

"The library," Wiglaf said.

"Yes, yes," Mordred said. "Brother Dave up in the library will copy it over. Then I shall send it off to Belcheena."

Wiglaf's hand shook as he held the letter:

Wednesday, June 8

To Her Royal ~~Richness~~ Highness,

Princess Bil~~lions~~ Belcheena, Mildew Palace, East Armpittsia

Dear Princess ~~Bil~~ Belcheena:

I have read of your search for a husband. I know

such a ~~boy~~ ~~man~~ ~~twerp~~ person as you describe. He has killed two dragons. His hair is red. His name is Wiglaf of Pinwick.

As you can see, he meets all your requirements. So come and marry him. Do not delay. His heart ~~thumps~~ ~~clonks~~ ~~pounds~~ ~~beats~~ pitter-patters with love for you already.

Your number one matchmaker,

Mordred the Marvelous, Headmaster DSA

P.S. Wiglaf is perfect for you. So go ahead and bring along that great big pot of gold.

Wiglaf's heart indeed thumped, clonked, pounded, beat, and pitter-pattered. Not with love. But with fear that this awful thing might really happen!

Lobelia skimmed the letter. "Very nice, Mordie," she said when she finished.

Mordred smiled. He pulled a velvet bell cord hanging on the wall. A DSA student teacher quickly appeared at the door.

"Take this to Brother Dave." Mordred handed him the letter. "Wait while he copies it. Then give the copy to my scout, Yorick. Tell him to deliver it to Mildew Palace tonight."

Tonight! Wiglaf gulped. Things were moving quickly. Way too quickly!

"Now for the wedding plans!" Lobelia held up a list she had made. "The wedding shall take place in the rose garden," she said.

Mordred frowned. "What rose garden?"

"The one I shall plant in the castle yard," Lobelia replied. "I'm thinking red roses to go with the redhead theme. After the wedding, we'll have the feast. Frypot and I planned a menu to go with Belcheena's favorite letter—*W*. We're serving whitefish, Welsh rarebit, wolf chops, weasel tenderloin, wrens and warblers baked in a pie, watermelon, and wine. But Mordie, this will not come cheap."

"Spare no expense!" Mordred said. "A

princess must have a proper wedding. And surely Belcheena will pay for the whole shebang!"

Lobelia nodded. "Now, Wiglaf, you must pick a best man. Your most trusted friend in the world. One to stand by you as you say your vows."

"You should choose someone important," Mordred said. "Someone powerful. Someone...like me."

Wiglaf rolled his eyes. Mordred was the cause of this mess. He would never pick him. Angus and Erica were his good friends. But his most trusted friend in the world? That was his pig, Daisy. Wiglaf almost laughed, thinking what Mordred and Lobelia would say if he suggested that Daisy be in the wedding. A best pig! They would think he had lost his mind!

And suddenly Wiglaf realized that's just what he *would* say! If Mordred and Lobelia thought he was crazy, maybe they would give up trying to make him marry the princess.

"My best friend must stand by me!" Wiglaf declared.

"Fine," Lobelia said. "Just tell me his name. I will have him measured for a new tunic."

"It is a she," Wiglaf said. "My pig, Daisy."

"Your pig? Over my dead body!" Mordred roared.

"Daisy must stand by me!" Wiglaf smiled strangely. He tried to look quite mad.

"I'll roast that pig of yours for the wedding supper!" Mordred roared.

"Stop, Mordie," Lobelia said. "Clearly the pig cannot be the best man. But picture this. Daisy as...the flower girl!"

"Have you lost your mind?" Mordred bellowed.

"Not her, me!" Wiglaf cried. "I'm the one who's lost my mind!"

"Shush!" Lobelia said. "A flower pig has

never been done. It's new. Cutting-edge! What a statement it would make!"

Panic gripped Wiglaf. He had not counted on this! How could Lobelia want a pig in a wedding? He had to do something fast.

"Yes! Here's the statement it would make!" Wiglaf said. And he started oinking like a pig.

"Stop that, Wiglaf," ordered Lobelia. "It would say our lives are connected to the earth. To beasts—the pig. This is such a fine idea," she added. "Perhaps the hens should be in the wedding, too."

"Ooooh! I feel a headache coming on!" Mordred groaned. "All right, Lobelia. Make what plans you will. But I warn you..." He raised one bushy eyebrow. "Don't do a thing that will put a stop to this wedding. For I shall let nothing—*nothing!*—stand between me and that pot of gold!"

Chapter 4

Wiglaf stumbled into the dorm room late that night. But Angus and Erica had waited up for him.

"What happened, Wiggie?" Erica whispered. "Did you talk Mordred out of this crazy idea?"

Wiglaf shook his head. "Mordred wrote Belcheena that he had found the perfect husband for her.... Me!" he wailed. "Yorick is on his way to Mildew Palace with the letter right now!"

"Well, look at the bright side," Angus advised. "You will be very rich."

"What do I care for riches?" Wiglaf moaned.

"You can order the best suit of armor from *The Sir Lancelot Catalog*," Erica pointed out. "And the ruby-handled sword!"

Wiglaf pictured the handsome ruby-handled sword from Erica's catalog. That part didn't sound so bad.

"No more lumpen pudding," Angus said. "And no more Scrubbing Class!"

"I hadn't thought about that," Wiglaf said.

"And someone will wait on you, hand and foot," Erica added. "You'll like that, Wiggie."

Wiglaf smiled. "That's *Prince* Wiggie to you!" Then his smile faded. "But I don't want to get mar... Oh, why did Mordred write that letter?"

"You know..." Angus said thoughtfully. "We, too, can write a letter."

Erica grinned. "Our letter could say how awful Wiglaf of Pinwick really is!"

"Yes!" Wiglaf cried. "Let us write it now!"

Erica ran off to her bunk. She quickly returned with paper and a goose quill pen.

"You write it, Angus." She gave him the supplies. "You have the worst handwriting."

"All right," Angus agreed. He settled himself on the floor. "What shall I write?"

"Dear Princess Belcheena," Wiglaf began. "A greedy matchmaker wrote you of a redheaded dragon slayer, Wiglaf of Pinwick. He wrote that Wiglaf would make you a perfect husband. Nothing could be further from the truth!"

"Let me add a bit," Erica said. And she took over. "You will know Wiglaf when you see him by the handsome wart on the tip of his nose. His lips are always nicely moist, for his drooling keeps them wet. Are you fond of dogs? I ask, for Wiglaf's breath is so like that of a hound. His teeth are artistically arranged. Some lean to the left. Others to the right. Still others lean way out of his mouth."

"Enough about my looks," Wiglaf said quickly.

Erica nodded. "Wiglaf would rather walk a mile on burning coals than marry you," she went on. "But he is a fortune hunter. And you have a fortune. So he shall wed you for your gold." Erica smiled. "That is enough, I think."

Wiglaf took the pen. He signed the letter, "From a True Friend at DSA." He blew on the ink to dry it. Then he rolled the letter up. Erica tied it with a ribbon.

"Let us keep this mar...mar...this thing a secret," Wiglaf suggested. "I have no wish for the other students here to know about it."

"I shan't say a word," Angus promised.

"Me either," Erica said. "I swear it on my genuine Sir Lancelot sword!"

The three friends locked pinkies to seal their promise.

"Maybe Yorick is back from Mildew Palace by now," Erica said. "Let's go see."

They tiptoed out of the dorm. They ran

silently through the hallways and across the castle yard. Wiglaf opened the door to the gatehouse. But it was empty except for a large rock on a pile of straw.

"Too bad," Angus said. "Yorick isn't here."

Suddenly the rock sat up. A hand reached out and slipped off a gray hood.

"Yorick!" Wiglaf exclaimed. "We thought you were a rock."

"That's the idea," Yorick said, getting to his feet. "This is my rock disguise—gray tights, a gray tunic, gray hood. When I spot trouble, I squat down by the side of the road. People take me for a rock and walk on by."

"We have a letter, Yorick," Wiglaf said. "It must be delivered to Mildew Palace right away."

"I just got back from there!" Yorick exclaimed. "I'm not going again so soon. Not on your life."

"I shall pay you a penny," Angus offered.

"No, Angus!" Wiglaf cried. "Your mother gave you that penny for your birthday!"

"It's a small price to pay to keep you from getting married and— oops!" Angus clapped a hand to his mouth.

"Wiglaf's getting married?" Yorick asked.

"Not if I can help it," Wiglaf said quickly. "That's why we need you to take this letter."

Angus gave Yorick the penny. Yorick bit down on it to make sure it was real.

"I'm off!" Yorick took the letter from Wiglaf. He tucked it into his tunic. And he hurried away.

Tomorrow morning, Wiglaf thought, *Princess Belcheena will read this letter. And she will never want to lay eyes on Wiglaf of Pinwick!*

Wiglaf, Angus, and Erica started back across the yard. They had almost reached the castle when a voice called: "Halt! Who goes there?"

Wiglaf froze. So did Angus and Erica.

"Oh, it's you three," the voice said. It belonged to Coach Plungett. "I thought I'd caught a pack of thieves on my watch," Coach said with a chuckle. He put his sword away. "What are you lads doing out here at this time of night?"

"We...uh," Wiglaf began. "We were just..."

"We couldn't sleep," Erica put in.

"Couldn't sleep, eh?" Coach looked up at the starry sky. "I once suffered from sleepless nights," he said. "It was long ago. I couldn't sleep for thinking of my lady love."

"You were in love!" Angus cried. "Yuck!"

Wiglaf smiled. It was funny to think of Coach Plungett in love. And yet...Coach had never married. How had he escaped?

"Excuse me, Coach?" Wiglaf said. "If I may ask—how is it you never mar...mar..."

"Married?" Coach said. "I was a lowly squire and my lady love's father thought I'd never amount to a hill of beans. One night he sent his henchmen to tell me to go. Said they'd stab me full of holes if I returned. There were twenty of them. And only one of me. So I rode off. I thought it best at the time." Coach sighed. "But sometimes I wonder, lads."

Wiglaf sighed, too. Clearly Coach's story was no help to him.

"That's a sad tale, Coach," said Angus.

"'Tis," Coach agreed. "Now go in and get some sleep. I won't be in class for a few days, you know. I'm off to Ratswhiskers to visit my mother. Sir Mort will take over for me. He'll be showing you the Fatal Blow."

"Good night, Coach," the three called. Then they headed for the castle.

Wiglaf had a light heart all day on Thursday. He pictured the princess opening the second letter. And crossing Wiglaf of

Pinwick off her list of possible husbands.

Friday morning, Wiglaf, Erica, and Angus walked into the dining hall for breakfast. Wiglaf caught sight of Mordred. He was running toward him, waving a piece of parchment. The headmaster was smiling broadly. This was not a good sign.

"Princess Belcheena has written back!" Mordred exclaimed as he reached Wiglaf.

Wiglaf's heart began to pound. Something was amiss. He could feel it in his bones.

"Her steward brought her reply this morning," Mordred went on. "Listen to what she says!"

Wiglaf looked nervously around the dining hall. All the boys had stopped eating. They were silent, waiting to hear more.

"*My dear Mordred,*" Mordred read loudly. "*How kind of you to write to let me know that Wiglaf of Pinwick would make me such a fine husband!*"

"Woo! Woo! Woo!" shouted all the boys in the dining hall. "Wiglaf's getting married!"

"Silence!" Mordred roared. His violet eyes flashed with anger. He read on.

"*I shall gladly come to Dragon Slayers' Academy to meet this redheaded dragon slayer. Please have your best room ready for me.*' Then she says something about even if I have to move out of the best room myself...clean sheets, blah, blah, blah. Let me see..." His eyes traveled down the page. "Ah! *I shall arrive on Saturday with my ladies-in-waiting, servants, and hangers-on. If Wiglaf is as perfect as you say, we shall be wed the following Saturday. I shall, of course, bring the pot of gold.*

Sincerely,

Princess Belcheena, Mildew Palace.'"

"Let us be wed, Wiglaf, honey!" called a boy.

Wiglaf's face burned hot with shame.

"She'll bring her gold!" Mordred exclaimed.

"That is the main thing. And she will be here tomorrow! Oh, there is much to do!"

Wiglaf tried to think. Belcheena must have sent this letter before she received the second one. Yes, that was it. Surely Mordred would soon get a second letter from Belcheena. And this one would say she was not coming after all.

"We must hurry!" Mordred said over the jeering boys. "We can't have Belcheena backing out of the deal when she lays eyes on you, Wiglaf. Come!" He grabbed Wiglaf's arm. "We must get you to Lobelia right away! She'll teach you manners. Show you how to eat with a knife, the way proper folks do. She'll show you how to bow. And most important, how to kiss the princess's hand."

The last thing Wiglaf heard as Mordred dragged him from the dining hall was boys making loud, juicy kissing sounds.

Chapter 5

"Sister!" Mordred cried. He flung Wiglaf into Lobelia's chamber. "Teach this riffraff some manners. And quickly! Belcheena is coming tomorrow. We can't have her refusing to marry the boy because he acts like a peasant."

"Tomorrow!" Lobelia gasped. "We don't have a moment to lose! Kneel down, Wiglaf. For you must kneel when you first speak to the princess."

Wiglaf fell to his knees.

"Start by praising Belcheena," Lobelia said. "Tell her she has lovely eyes and hair and lips. Make your bride-to-be feel beautiful!"

"Uh...beautiful Belcheena," Wiglaf began. "You have hair. And...uh, teeth..."

"Oh, for goodness' sakes!" Mordred cried. "Like this!" The big man dropped to his knees. He clasped his hands together. He blinked his violet eyes. "Oh, my lovely billionairess...er, I mean, princess!" he said. "Your hair shines like pure gold in the sunlight. Your eyes are as blue as sapphires! Your teeth are as bright as freshly minted coins!"

Wiglaf tried again. "Oh, Princess, your skin is as soft...as...as a sheep's belly."

"Not a sheep's belly!" Mordred bellowed.

"A sheep's belly *is* very soft," Wiglaf said.

"But not terribly romantic," Lobelia pointed out. "Say soft as a cloud."

After the praising lesson, Lobelia sat Wiglaf down. He practiced keeping his elbows off the table. He practiced drinking from a goblet without slurping. All the while, Lobelia read to him from *Medieval Manners: Do's and Don't's*.

"'Don't spit in your plate during dinner,'"

she read. "'Wait until the meal is finished. Don't pick your teeth with your knife—always use the point of your sword. Don't blow your nose on the hem of the tablecloth. Use your sleeve.'"

Lobelia kept at it all morning. She dismissed Wiglaf for lunch, telling him to practice his manners in the dining hall. Wiglaf's head spun with do's and don't's as he carried his tray to the Class I table.

"Wiglaf!" Erica exclaimed as he sat down. "I have good news!"

"What?" Wiglaf's heart leapt with hope. "Has Yorick returned with an answer from Belcheena?"

"No. But my order from *The Sir Lancelot Catalog* came!" Erica announced.

Wiglaf's heart sank. "That's nice," he managed.

"Here," Erica said. "I want you to have this." She pressed a ring into his hand. It had a milky blue stone. "It's a Sir Lancelot almost-magic foretelling ring," she explained. "When the stone is blue, all is well. But if it turns orange and starts blinking, it means *danger, danger, danger!*"

Wiglaf slipped the ring onto the first finger of his left hand. The stone's blue glow comforted him somehow. He thanked Erica.

"After lunch, let's go find Yorick," Angus suggested. "Maybe he has brought back Belcheena's reply. And surely that will be good news."

They found Yorick outside the henhouse. He was gathering feathers for his pigeon disguise.

"Yorick!" Wiglaf called. "Did you give Princess Belcheena the letter?"

"Uh...thieves set upon me!" Yorick cried.

"Didn't you squat down on the side of the road and pretend to be a rock?" Angus asked.

"Of course I did!" Yorick said. "But the

thieves thought I *was* a rock. So they sat on me! I let out a cry. And the next thing I knew, they were robbing me! Took my penny, they did. So here." Yorick pulled the letter from his tunic and gave it to Wiglaf. "I knew you wouldn't want me delivering it without my proper pay."

Wiglaf groaned. Here was his last chance to keep Belcheena from coming to DSA—ruined! He crumpled the letter into a ball.

Erica patted Wiglaf on the back. "Don't worry, Wiggie," she said. "Look. Your ring is still blue. There is no danger. Everything will turn out all right. Come! Let us be off to Slaying Class. Sir Mort is teaching us today."

"I shall be there in a minute," Wiglaf told his friends. "First I must go see Daisy."

Wiglaf walked to the henhouse.

"Daisy?" he called. "Are you here, girl?"

Daisy came trotting out to meet Wiglaf.

"Ello-hay, Iggie-way!" she exclaimed.

Wiglaf knelt down. He put his arms around his pig and hugged her.

"I can't stay long, Daisy," he said. "But I had to see you. For alas! Mordred is trying to make me get mar...mar..." No sound came out. But he managed to mouth the word.

Daisy gasped. "Arried-may?"

Wiglaf nodded. Then he poured his heart out to his pig. "I even tried to get out of it by saying that you must be in the wedding," Wiglaf added.

"Eally-ray?" Daisy said brightly.

Wiglaf nodded. "But Lobelia liked the idea! She wants you to be the flower pig!"

"I-yay ould-way ove-lay o-tay!" Daisy said.

"No, no!" Wiglaf cried. "I don't want to get mar... I want things to stay just as they are!"

"Illy-say oy-bay!" Daisy exclaimed. "I-yay ove-lay eddings-way!"

Wiglaf moaned. Daisy didn't seem to understand. He had counted on his wise pig to help him. He had never guessed that Daisy was so very fond of weddings.

"E-may, a-yay ower-flay ig-pay!" Daisy burbled happily. "Is-thay is-yay e-thay appiest-hay ay-day of-yay y-may ife-lay!"

"I must go to Slaying, Daisy." Wiglaf stood up. He rubbed his pig on her head. Then he stumbled from the henhouse in a daze.

Slaying Class went badly for Wiglaf that afternoon. He was late, for one thing. And he never had gotten the homework from Torblad. Sir Mort called on him to name three spots on a dragon where a dragon slayer could strike a fatal blow. But he could not name even one. The old knight looked very disappointed.

When at last class ended, Wiglaf ran over to Angus and Erica.

"I have an idea," he whispered to them. "For getting out of getting mar...mar... For getting out of this mess. I shall call Zelnoc!"

"That crazy wizard?" Angus asked. "The one who messed up Daisy's speech spell?"

"He's not very good," Wiglaf admitted. "But he *is* a wizard. Surely he must have some magic that can help me."

"We have a break before Alchemy Class," Erica said. "Let us summon this enchanter now."

"I know a secret part of the dungeon," Angus added. "No one ever goes there."

"Perfect," Wiglaf said. "Let's go there now. For my time is running out!"

Chapter 6

Wiglaf, Angus, and Erica ran down the stone stairway to the dungeon. Angus led them to a damp room way at the back. A tiny window near the ceiling let in the only light.

Wiglaf closed his eyes. He chanted Zelnoc's name backwards three times: "Conlez, Conlez, Conlez."

A faint breeze tickled Wiglaf's cheek. He opened his eyes. A puff of smoke was rising from the floor. The puff grew and grew until the room was filled with thick black smoke.

Wiglaf's eyes began to water.

Angus and Erica started coughing.

Then suddenly, out of the smoke, leapt a

white rabbit. It was followed by another. And another. Before long, dozens of the furry creatures were hopping around the dungeon.

"Zelnoc?" Wiglaf called. "Are you here?"

"Of course I am!" boomed a voice inside the smoke. "I was summoned, was I not?"

With that, the smoke lifted. And there stood a wizard. He wore a dark blue pointed hat and robe, dotted with silver stars.

"Whoa!" Angus said. He and Erica backed up.

Zelnoc stepped forward, tripping over a rabbit.

"Blasted bunnies!" he cursed. "How was I to know that saying *Bibbity Babbit* summoned rabbits? I thought I was doing a wart removal chant. So, it's you, is it, Weglip?"

"Yes, sir." Wiglaf began to worry. He had forgotten how mixed up Zelnoc's spells could get. "These are my friends, Eric and Angus."

"Charmed," Zelnoc said. "Do either of you know a spell for getting rid of rabbits?"

Erica and Angus shook their heads.

"I didn't think so," Zelnoc said miserably. He turned to Wiglaf. "So, what'll it be this time, Wigloaf? Another courage spell?"

"No, sir," Wiglaf said. "I need a spell so I won't have to get mar...mar..."

"Married," Angus put in. "My Uncle Mordred is arranging for him to marry Princess Belcheena."

"A princess, eh?" Zelnoc exclaimed. "Good work, my boy! Princesses don't usually go for you peasant types."

"I don't want her to go for me," Wiglaf exclaimed. "I called you to get me out of it!"

"No problem," Zelnoc said. "I'll brew you an anti-love potion. Belcheena takes a few sips of it and—zowie! The first person she lays eyes on, she shall hate with all her might."

"That sounds perfect!" Wiglaf said. "And I shall make certain that person is *me!*"

"Tell me, wizard," Erica said. "What do you put into such a potion?"

"A pinch of pepper, six hairs from a skunk tail, a lump of lumpen pudding," Zelnoc said. "I can't tell the whole recipe, of course. That would be breaking Wizard Rule #457. But it's a doozie."

"When can I have it?" Wiglaf asked.

"Let me think...." The wizard tapped his fingers on his chin. "Two weeks from today."

"Alas!" Wiglaf cried. "Then I am doomed!"

"The wedding is to take place next Saturday," Angus explained.

"Why didn't you say it was a rush job?" asked Zelnoc. "Nothing is impossible! We wizards always have a trick up our sleeves!"

To prove his point, Zelnoc reached up his sleeve. He pulled out...a rabbit.

"Egad!" he cried as the bunny jumped from his hand. "I'm having a really bad hare day!"

"Is there nothing else you can do for Wiglaf, sir?" asked Erica.

"There is always something else," Zelnoc said. "I'll give Waglom a smelling spell. It's like perfume—with a kick. Let me see.... Ah! I know! Whiff of Loathing. That's the ticket. One sniff, and bingo! Belcheena will detest you forever! Or at least until the spell wears off. Never fear! I shall bring it soon. Now, I must get back to my tower and figure out how to get rid of these rabbits."

"Oh, thank you, sir!" Wiglaf said, as, once more, the dungeon filled with smoke.

"Farewell, Wugloom!" Zelnoc called. "Come, bunnies! Hop to it!"

The rabbits jumped into the smoke with Zelnoc. Then, one and all, they disappeared.

Wiglaf ran happily up the dungeon stairs after Erica and Angus. Summoning Zelnoc had been a good idea after all! At the top of the stairs, they bumped into Mordred.

"Wiglaf!" the headmaster boomed. "I've been looking for you." He sniffed. "Do I smell smoke?"

"Frypot must have burned the lumpen pudding again," Angus said quickly.

"Ah, yes," Mordred said. "Come, Wiglaf! Lobelia is waiting!"

"But sir!" Wiglaf said. "I have to go to Alchemy Class."

"Classes are canceled," Mordred said. "Except for Scrubbing. Eric and Angus, you missed the sign-up. So you'll have to scrub the privy. Wiglaf, you go to Lobelia's. She's waiting to give you a makeover."

"A...what?" Wiglaf said.

"Lobelia wants you to look your best when you meet Belcheena tomorrow," Mordred said. "So go!"

Wiglaf hurried down the hallway. To his

horror, he saw that the stone in his ring was turning orange. It started blinking: *danger, danger, danger!* His heart pounded. This was not a good sign.

"Wiglaf!" Lobelia exclaimed as she waved him into her chamber. "I found the most charming drawing of Prince Putroc in *Royal Lads Magazine.* Just feast your eyes on his hair!" Lobelia held up the drawing. Prince Putroc's hair hung down on his forehead in ringlet curls. "You, Wiglaf, will look royal when I've curled your hair."

"*My* hair?" Wiglaf cried. No wonder his ring had been blinking! "No! Please! That picture is...awful!"

"Trust me on this, Wiglaf," Lobelia said. "Those curls are *you!* But we have a few other things to take care of first. Sit on that stool."

Wiglaf sat. Lobelia began spreading foul-smelling green goo all over his face.

"This clay is from Dead Fish Swamp. It does wonders for the skin. There." She stepped back to see if she had missed any spots.

Wiglaf felt the clay hardening.

"Now tilt your head back," Lobelia said.

Wiglaf did as he was told.

"Cucumbers take away puffiness." She pressed two big slices over his eyes.

Wiglaf felt the juice trickling into his ears.

"And for your lips," Lobelia added, "pepper paste." She smeared some on.

"Yow!" Wiglaf yelped. "It stings!"

"That's what brings out the nice rosy color," Lobelia explained. "Try not to lick your lips."

Wiglaf wanted to ask how long he must have all this disgusting stuff on him. But he was afraid to open his mouth.

"You know your ears stick out, don't you, Wiglaf?" Lobelia went on. "Well, I'm told that half an onion will draw the ear closer to the head." She hung half an onion from a string on each of Wiglaf's ears.

"Now hold still while I work on your fingernails," Lobelia said. "Rough hands are the sign of a peasant. Maybe you should wear gloves."

When she finished his nails, Lobelia began wrapping strands of Wiglaf's hair around a red-hot curling iron.

Wiglaf had faced two fire-breathing dragons. They had not killed him. But he thought Lobelia might. Certainly she was skilled at torture.

It seemed to Wiglaf that his makeover took forever. But at last he found his way back to the dorm room. He had a nasty rash on his cheeks from the swamp clay. His lips burned a fiery red. Carrot-colored ringlets danced on his forehead.

"Wiglaf!" Erica exclaimed when she saw him. "Have you caught the plague?"

"I wish," Wiglaf moaned. "Death by plague must be better than a makeover!" He flopped down on his cot. "And the worst is yet to come. Belcheena arrives tomorrow."

"We have to help him, Angus," Erica said.

"We do," Angus agreed. "But how?"

"How indeed." Erica tapped her foot as she thought. "I do have one idea," she said at last. "The Bag-o-Laughs Kit I ordered from *Junior Jester Magazine*. That should do the trick!"

"Oh, I think I saw some of the stuff you got...like the flower that squirts water?" Angus said. "And the black gum that makes one's teeth appear to be missing? And the hand buzzer? And the fake doggie poo?"

"Yes!" Erica answered with a smile. "We shall give Belcheena a very special welcome indeed!"

Chapter 7

On Saturday morning, Wiglaf opened his eyes. He checked his ring. It was blue now. But surely it would soon turn orange. For this was the day Belcheena was coming!

After breakfast, Wiglaf slowly made his way to Lobelia's chamber. He had just raised his hand to knock on the door, when a bright light flashed before him.

"Egad!" cried Wiglaf, jumping back.

In the spot where the light had been, Zelnoc shimmered into being.

"How do you like my new entrance?" the wizard asked. "I call it 'The Flash.' Beats the smoke, yes sir! I'm on a roll now, Waglop! I invented Bunnies-B-Gone. And poof! No more rabbits!"

"That's nice," Wiglaf said. "Did you bring me the loathing stuff?"

"Do bats have wings?" the wizard said. "Of course I did!" He reached up his sleeve and pulled out a bottle of bright red liquid.

"Are you sure it will work?" Wiglaf asked.

Zelnoc scowled down at Wiglaf. "Would I bring you something that didn't work?"

"Well..." Wiglaf didn't know how to put it. Zelnoc's spells had a way of turning out badly.

Just then, Lobelia opened her door.

"Hello, Wiglaf," she said. Then she looked at Zelnoc. "A wizard!" she exclaimed. "But why are you dressed in that old robe?"

Zelnoc frowned. "What's wrong with it?"

"That star pattern is *so* last year," Lobelia said. "Wizards nowadays go in for comets, meteor showers, shooting stars. They want a

powerful image. But come in, both of you."
She smiled. "I have a surprise for Wiglaf."

A surprise? Wiglaf had had more than
enough of those. But he followed Zelnoc into
Lobelia's chamber. And there was Daisy.

Wiglaf stared. His pig wore a pink silk cape.
A crown of tiny rosebuds sat on her head.

"Why are you dressed up?" Zelnoc asked.

"Iglaf-way's edding-way," Daisy said.

"Ah, yes. The wedding." Zelnoc winked at
Wiglaf. "That's why I'm here, too, in a way."

Lobelia gasped. "Wiglaf, that's brilliant!"
she cried. "A wizard in your wedding!"

"No, no, no," Zelnoc said. "Wizard Rule
#45 clearly states *no wizards in weddings*.
Funerals, sometimes. But weddings? Never."

"Oh, rules were made to be broken,"
Lobelia scoffed. She began circling Zelnoc.
"I'll trim your beard and find you a new robe.
One that will make you *look* powerful, even if
your powers aren't up to scratch."

"What?" Zelnoc cried. "My powers are just fine, thank you very much."

"Don't get huffy," Lobelia said.

"Huffy?" Zelnoc exclaimed. "Wizards don't get huffy! Wizards get *angry!* Wizards get *even!* Especially mighty, powerful wizards, like me!"

"Oh, puh-leeze!" Lobelia exclaimed.

Zelnoc popped the cork on the bottle of red potion.

"Doubt my powers, will you?" Zelnoc snarled. "Well, let's have a little test."

He waved the bottle under Lobelia's nose.

Wiglaf watched in horror as Lobelia's violet eyes began rolling around in circles.

"What have you done?" Wiglaf cried.

Lobelia's eyes closed. Then they popped open. Lobelia stared at Zelnoc.

"Well?" the wizard said eagerly. "You hate me with all your heart, don't you?"

She clasped her hands to her chest and cried,

"*Oh, say not such a cruel thing!*
With love for you my heart does sing!"

"Uh-oh," said Zelnoc.

Lobelia went on:

"*Your wizard's hat is such a tall one!*
In love with you I must have fallen!"

"E-shay oves lay ou-yay!" Daisy sang happily.

"This is worse than rabbits!" Zelnoc cried.

Lobelia continued:

"*Oh, Wizard, though you're old and wrinkled,*
With love for you my heart is sprinkled!"

Wiglaf grabbed the bottle of red liquid from Zelnoc's hand. He read the tiny printing on the label: "Oil of Rhymes-o-Love."

"Oops," Zelnoc said. "I picked up the wrong bottle. But it works, Wuglop. You can see that, can't you? My spells do work!"

Lobelia took Zelnoc's hand in hers.

"*Wizard, with your beard so white!*
Dance with me in the pale moonlight!"

Zelnoc pulled his hand away. "Wizard Rule #498—*no dancing*. I'm getting out of here!"

Lobelia cried,

"Oh, wizard, with your robe so blue,
If you leave, I'll cry: Boo hoo!"

Zelnoc turned to Wiglaf. "I'm gone," he said. And with a bright flash of light, he was.

Tears streamed down Lobelia's cheeks.

"My wizard, he is gone from me.
I cannot stand such misery!"

"You don't really love him, my lady," Wiglaf said weakly. "It's a spell. It will wear off."

But Lobelia would not be comforted. She cried and sobbed and carried on. At last she threw her velvet cloak around her shoulders.

"Where are you going?" Wiglaf asked.

Lobelia cried miserably:

"This pain I feel, I must be stopping!
There's just one cure—I'm going shopping!"

Chapter 8

Wiglaf sank onto Lobelia's couch. He should have known better than to call Zelnoc. Whiff of Loathing indeed!

"Oor-pay Obelia-lay!" Daisy exclaimed.

"Lobelia's spell will wear off," Wiglaf said. "But Belcheena will be mine forever!"

Mordred stuck his head in the door.

"Ah, here you are, Wiglaf!" he exclaimed. "Yorick has just spotted Princess Belcheena! She and her party are starting up Huntsman's Path. They will be here within the hour!"

"Woe is me!" Wiglaf groaned.

"Why are you not dressed?" Mordred asked. "And where is my sister?"

"Opping-shay," Daisy said.

"Shopping?" Mordred cried. "At a time like this? She must have gotten wind of that bodice sale over in Ratswhiskers. Well, never mind. Now where did she put that new outfit she ordered for you, Wiglaf? Ah, here it is!" Mordred picked up a package tied up with string. He thrust it into Wiglaf's hands.

Instantly, Wiglaf's ring begin to flash a bright orange warning.

"Go put it on!" Mordred roared.

Wiglaf shook as he ducked behind the tapestry. He was in danger! But what could he do? He took off his DSA uniform. He put on his new outfit.

"Don't dillydally, boy!" Mordred yelled.

Wiglaf quickly fastened the squirting flower that Erica had given him to the collar of his new tunic. He stuck the tooth-black gum into his pocket. He slipped the hand buzzer onto his palm. Then he stepped out from behind the tapestry.

Wiglaf yelped as he beheld himself in Lobelia's looking glass. No wonder his ring had signaled danger! For he wore a swamp-green velvet tunic. His skinny legs, in matching tights, looked like toothpicks. His shoes had long, curled-up toes!

Mordred set a swamp-green mushroom-shaped hat on top of Wiglaf's ringlets. "There!" he said. "The hat gives you a lordly look."

"Ery-vay oble-nay!" Daisy exclaimed.

Wiglaf didn't think "noble" was quite the right word. The right word was "ninny." He looked like some half-witted elf!

Wiglaf stared at himself. And then he smiled. Surely Princess Belcheena would never marry anyone who looked this foolish!

"Come!" Mordred said. "It is time for you to go to the castle yard to greet your bride!"

Wiglaf's shoes flapped as he followed Mordred outside.

Every DSA student stood in the castle yard, waiting to see the East Armpittsian princess.

Wiglaf heard giggles as he passed by.

"Look at mushroom head!" called a boy.

"Hey, string bean legs!" called another.

But Wiglaf walked with his head held high. So what if they laughed? If the silly outfit saved him from marrying Belcheena, he would gladly wear it for the rest of his life.

Wiglaf spotted Angus and Erica in the crowd. But he could only wave to them and walk on.

Suddenly trumpets sounded. And Yorick cried, "Her Royal Highness, Princess Belcheena!"

Then through the castle gates marched a juggler juggling oranges. He was followed by two jesters turning cartwheels. Three minstrels strolled in next, strumming their lutes and singing. Four ladies-in-waiting were followed by five servants. The last one held the leash of a fierce-looking wild boar with golden tips on his tusks.

Wiglaf had never seen such a glorious parade. If only he did not know who was at the end of it.

Now a team of six horses pulled a golden carriage through the gate. And waving from the window was none other than Princess Belcheena.

"Welcome to Dragon Slayers' Academy!" Mordred boomed. He nodded to the DSA band. The boys struck up a squeaky tune.

Wiglaf watched with growing dread as the servants opened the carriage door. The ladies-in-waiting helped Princess Belcheena out.

Belcheena was a large princess. Much larger than Wiglaf had expected. A pointed hat sat on her head. A long lacy scarf trailed down from its tip. Her braided yellow hair hung down nearly to her knees.

"Welcome, Princess!" Mordred said. "As headmaster of this fine academy, I welcome—"

"Stop!" Princess Belcheena cried.

Mordred stopped midspeech.

"Well, where is he?" the princess said loudly. "Where is this Wiglaf of Pinwick?"

"Right here, your loadedness!" Mordred said. "I mean, your loveliness! Go on, boy!" He gave Wiglaf a push. "Do as I taught you."

Wiglaf lurched forward.

"Look, Gretta," Belcheena said to the lady-in-waiting at her side. "His hair is not really red at all. I would call it orange."

Yes! Wiglaf thought. Belcheena wanted a truly redheaded husband. And he did not fill the bill!

"It is indeed orange," Wiglaf agreed.

To his surprise, the princess smiled. "My long-lost love had red-orange hair," she said. She plucked up a locket she wore on a chain around her neck. She opened it and sighed. "This is all I have left of him. A curl of his carroty hair!"

Wiglaf's face fell. This was not working out at all. She liked his stupid hair! But he wasn't giving up yet.

"Go on, Wiglaf. Compliment her," Mordred whispered.

Wiglaf stepped toward the princess.

"Beautiful Belcheena," he said. "You smell as sweet as the flower I wear on my tunic!"

Belcheena leaned forward to smell the flower. Wiglaf pushed a little bulb in his pocket. *Spuuuurt!* The flower squirted Belcheena's face.

"Aaack!" cried the surprised princess.

"My lady!" screamed Gretta. She began patting Belcheena's cheeks dry with her handkerchief.

Before the princess could recover, Wiglaf struck again. "Princess Belcheena," he said. "Let me kiss your hand!"

He took Belcheena's hand in his and squeezed.

The hand buzzer sounded: *Buzzzzzzzzzz!*

"Yowie!" Belcheena cried. She jumped back.

Mordred rushed over to Belcheena.

"Princess!" he cried. "I shall have Wiglaf flogged! I'll put him in the Thumb Screws. I'll put him in the Foot Smasher. I'll put him in the Limb Stretcher until his arms are six feet long!"

"Shush!" Belcheena waved Mordred away. She eyed Wiglaf. "I was not expecting that!" she said.

Wiglaf smiled broadly.

"Please forgive Wiglaf, Princess!" Mordred cried. "I shall throw him in the dungeon! But of course, you will still marry him, won't you? You'll still give me that great big pot of gold?"

"Scat!" Belcheena yelled at Mordred.

The headmaster slunk away.

"Tell me, Wiglaf of Pinwick!" Belcheena said. "The squirting flower and the hand buzzer...are they from the Junior Jester Bag-o-Laughs Kit?"

The question caught Wiglaf by surprise.

"Why, yes, they are, my lady," he answered.

"Ha!" Belcheena cried. She gave Wiglaf a hearty slap on the back. "There's nothing I like better than a practical joke!" She grinned. "I, too, ordered the Bag-o-Laughs! I was going to have some fun with you! Just look!"

Belcheena slipped her hand into the pocket of her gown. She brought her hand to her mouth. Then she smiled, and her two front teeth appeared to be missing.

Belcheena threw back her head and roared with laughter. She gave Wiglaf another mighty slap. This one sent him sprawling face-down in the castle yard.

"You are not half the man my long-lost love was," the princess said as Wiglaf struggled to his feet. "Not even a quarter, really. But you're a rascal! Oh, what fine times we shall have at Mildew Palace!"

"You...you like him then?" Mordred asked. "You still want to marry Wiglaf?"

"Why not?" Belcheena boomed. "And why wait a week? Let us be wed tomorrow!"

"But...but...but..." Wiglaf sputtered.

He was drowned out by Mordred. "Oh, joy! Oh, golden day!" the headmaster cried. "By the way, your royal richness. I mean, highness...about that pot of gold."

Princess Belcheena rolled her eyes. "Is that all you can think of?" she asked.

"Well, frankly...yes," Mordred mumbled. "I mean, no! Of course not!"

"Good," said the princess. "Now, I have had

a hard journey to this forsaken part of the kingdom. I want to rest. Is your very best room ready for me?"

"Yes, Princess!" Mordred said. "Yorick!" he called. "Show the princess to her room!"

"Ta ta, Wigs!" Belcheena wiggled her fingers at him. "Wait! What is that on your head?"

"What?" said Wiglaf. He swatted at his hair.

"This." Belcheena reached out and seemed to pluck something from the top of his head. She held it out in front of him.

It was a...a human thumb! Blood was caked around its base where it had been cut from a hand! Wiglaf swayed dizzily, just looking at it.

"Ha!" Belcheena cackled. "Gotcha, Wigs!"

She tossed the horrid thumb to him. It was made of rubber. Then she skipped merrily into the castle.

"Back to class, boys!" Mordred cried. "We'll celebrate tonight at Wiglaf's bachelor party!"

"Hooray!" the students cheered.

Angus and Erica ran over to Wiglaf. "I'm doomed!" Wiglaf cried.

"No, you're not," Erica said. "Look at your ring. The stone is still blue."

But Wiglaf was losing faith in his ring. "Here," he said, handing the thumb to Erica.

"Thanks!" Erica exclaimed. "The severed thumb only comes in the super-duper Bag-o-Laughs. You get a whoopie cushion with that one, too."

"That's nice," said Wiglaf. But he wasn't thinking about whoopie cushions. Or severed thumbs. He was thinking of Princess Belcheena. And how he was going to be spending the rest of his life with her.

Chapter 9

"Three cheers for the groom!" Mordred boomed as Wiglaf walked into the dining hall for his bachelor party that night.

"Hip, hip, hooray!" everyone cried three times.

The room was hung with greenery. Platters of steaming food lined the tables. There wasn't a bowl of lumpen pudding in sight.

Wiglaf sat in the seat of honor. Angus and Erica sat on either side of him. They dug into the dinner. But Wiglaf could not eat a bite.

Mordred strolled by. "Eat up, Wiglaf!" he roared. "I've spared no expense. Ah, what fun it is to spend the princess's money!" He clapped

Wiglaf on the back. "Have you picked a best man yet, my boy?"

Wiglaf turned to Angus. "Would you?" he asked.

"Honored," Angus said, with his mouth full.

During dinner, the juggler juggled. The minstrels sang. The boar was led around the room so that all might admire his fine gold-tipped tusks. Wiglaf would have enjoyed himself tremendously if only there had been another reason for the party.

Coach Plungett stood up to give a toast. He raised his flask. "Word reached me at my mother's cottage in Ratswhiskers that you were getting married, Wiglaf," he said. "I rushed back to wish you all the happiness in the world! Love is a wonderful thing, lad. Why, thinking of my long-lost lady love still makes my heart beat with joy. Some would say that I have been unlucky in love. Yet I say—not so! For a while, my lady love and I were as happy as pigs in a mud wallow. I remember the time..."

"Give your toast and sit down, Wendell!" Frypot called. "We don't want to be here all night!"

"To Wiglaf and his bride!" Coach said.

"Here! Here!" everyone shouted. "To Wiglaf and Belcheena!"

"Belcheena?" Suddenly, Coach choked on his mead and started coughing. Mordred had to slap him on the back for quite a while before the big man recovered.

Brother Dave gave the last toast of the evening. "Sleep well tonight, Wiglaf," the monk said. "For tomorrow when thou hearest wedding bells, they shall be ringing for thee!"

"I...I do," Wiglaf stuttered. He stood just

inside the door of the DSA castle, between his best man Angus and Mordred.

"Louder!" Mordred barked.

"I do!" Wiglaf shouted miserably.

Angus patted his shoulder.

The wedding was about to begin. Wiglaf pulled the scratchy pleated white collar away from his neck. Why did he have to wear the silly thing? Wasn't he in enough pain already?

A wedding day was supposed to be a happy day. But Wiglaf felt like crying. He did not want to leave his friends. He did not want to live in Mildew Palace with that prankster Belcheena. He did not even want to help her spend her billions.

"Once more," Mordred commanded.

"I dooooo!" wailed Wiglaf.

"That's better!" Mordred said.

Suddenly Lobelia rushed into the castle. She was loaded down with shopping bags.

"Oh, thank goodness!" she cried. "I made it back in time. I don't know what came over me, rushing off like that. Mordie, go check on Dr. Pluck. Tell him to start playing the organ!"

Mordred hurried off.

Lobelia uncapped a bottle from one of her bags. She squirted a sweet-smelling liquid on Wiglaf. "It's Groom Perfume," she said. "Isn't it wild? I'd better check on the bridesmaids now. I'll be back." And off she rushed.

Yuck! Now Wiglaf smelled just like a rose! He peeked out the door at Lobelia's rose-bushes. They were in full bloom. A cloth runner had been put down on the grass for Belcheena to walk on. Class III students were seating the wedding guests on long wooden benches.

Suddenly organ music started playing. Yikes! The wedding had begun!

Brother Dave walked out of the chapel. He stopped between the two biggest rosebushes.

"That is our signal," Angus whispered.

Wiglaf stood rooted to the spot.

"Come on!" Angus said. And he pulled the reluctant groom out into the castle yard.

Wiglaf blinked in the sunlight. He walked toward Brother Dave.

"Thou art doing fine, lad," the monk said when Wiglaf reached him.

Next came the wedding party, Gretta and the other ladies-in-waiting, with Daisy trotting behind them. She was wearing her pink silk cape. And her crown of rosebuds.

People gasped when they saw Daisy. They murmured to each other "Pig in a wedding!" and "What next?"

Now Dr. Pluck pounded on the organ keys and struck up "Here Comes the Bride."

Sir Mort began escorting Belcheena up the

runner. The princess wore a red gown. Her yellow braids were wound with ropes of pearls.

"So beautiful!" whispered the wedding guests. "Such a lovely dress!"

Wiglaf swallowed as the princess walked closer and closer to him. Her lips were bright pink. Her cheeks were rouged red. Blue shadow lined her eyelids. Wiglaf thought she looked scarier than any dragon.

Wiglaf found Erica's face in the crowd. She held up a finger. Wiglaf understood. He looked down at his ring. The stone was bright blue.

Phooey! he thought. The thing ought to be glowing like a red-hot coal! Clearly, *The Sir Lancelot Catalog* had sold Erica a dud.

Sir Mort walked Belcheena to her groom. He put the princess's arm on Wiglaf's. Then he bowed and took a seat in the front row beside Mordred.

Belcheena winked and smiled at Wiglaf.

Wiglaf tried to smile back.

"Dearly beloved," Brother Dave began. "We have come here today to join Belcheena Kristen Louise Wilhemina Bernadette Paula Frieda Marie, Princess of East Armpittsia and Wiglaf of Pinwick in marriage."

Wiglaf's knees began to shake.

"Steady, Wiglaf," Angus whispered.

"If any persons here know of a reason why these two people should not be joined in marriage," Brother Dave went on, "let them speak now, or forever hold their peace."

Silence filled the castle yard.

Brother Dave turned to Belcheena.

"Princess Belcheena," he said. "Do you take this—"

"Stop!" called a voice from the gatehouse. "Stop the wedding now!"

Chapter 10

The wedding guests gasped.

Wiglaf whirled around. His eyes searched the crowd.

"Look, there." Angus pointed toward the gatehouse. A tall man was making his way through the crowd.

Wiglaf gasped. "It's Coach Plungett!"

What is going on? he wondered.

Suddenly Belcheena let out a scream.

Wiglaf jumped.

Was this another one of Belcheena's jokes?

"Wendell!" Belcheena called. "Is it you?"

"Yes, Belchie? It is!" Coach Plungett cried.
He ran up to the princess. Belcheena slowly

held out her hand. Coach reached for it. But the princess quickly drew her hand away. "Gotcha!" she shrieked.

"Whoo-whoo!" Coach Plungett cried. "It's my rowdy old Belchie!" Then he picked her up and whirled her around and around.

"STOP THAT!" Mordred boomed.

Coach put the princess down.

"What, in the name of King Ken's britches, are you doing, Plungett?" Mordred roared.

"Gazing at my long-lost love," Coach replied. "Dearest Belchie!" he said. "I thought never to see you again!"

"Why did you leave me, Wendell? Why?" Belcheena asked.

"Your father's henchmen drove me from your palace," Coach Plungett said. "Many times I tried to return. But the guards kept me out. At last I went off questing in the Dark Forest. I tried to forget you, Belchie. But I never could."

"I never forgot you either," Belcheena said. "After you left, all I did was count my gold, order silly things from *Junior Jester Magazine*, and sing this song. Listen." And Belcheena began to sing.

> *"He set my heart on fire,*
> *That's the truth, I am no liar.*
> *When he left I was a crier*
> *For the Squire of My Desire!*
>
> *"Throughout the whole empire*
> *He's the one that I admire.*
> *There is no squire higher*
> *Than the Squire of My Desire!"*

"Oh, Belchie!" cried Coach.

"Sit down, Plungett," Mordred ordered. "You and Belcheena can talk about old times later. Now, let's get back to the wedding!"

But the princess and the coach paid no attention to the headmaster.

"I shall not lose you again, Belchie!" Coach Plungett vowed. He dropped to his knees and said, "Will you marry me?"

The princess smiled. She turned to Wiglaf. "I hope you don't mind terribly," she said, "but I must marry Wendell."

"So you must, Princess," Wiglaf said happily. "You must marry the one you love."

There. He'd said it: Marry!

"What will your father say?" Coach asked.

"Who cares?" the princess replied.

"Hold it! Hold it!" Mordred cried. "What about your conditions, Your Highness? True, Wendell Plungett is a dragon slayer. And his first name begins with *W*. But," Mordred added slyly, "he does not have red hair!"

"'Tis true," Coach Plungett said. He pulled off his wig. "I no longer have *any* hair."

"Who cares?" Princess Belcheena said again. "You once had lovely carrot-colored hair. I still carry a curl of it in my locket. That is enough for me."

Mordred groaned.

"I'll be your best man, Coach," Wiglaf offered.

Brother Dave began again. "Dearly beloved, we have come here today to join Princess Belcheena of Mildew Palace, East Armpittsia, and Wendell Plungett of Dragon Slayers' Academy in marriage."

What a celebration followed! No one had a better time than Wiglaf. He cheered for the jugglers. He sang along with the minstrels. He danced with Daisy. Later he smiled when he saw his pig in the crowd, flirting with the golden-tusked boar. He'd never been so happy.

"Look," said Angus at last. "The bride and groom are getting into the carriage."

"Let us bid them good-bye," Erica said.

Wiglaf, Angus, and Erica hurried over.

"Farewell, Coach!" Wiglaf said. "Farewell, Princess Belcheena!"

"Good-bye!" Belcheena called. "Come and visit us at Mildew Palace, won't you, Wigs? And bring your friends."

Mordred pushed his way to the carriage. "Excuse me, Princess," he said. "But as your matchmaker, I was wondering.... About that pot of gold?"

"Ah!" Belcheena said. "But I have not married Wiglaf of Pinwick. So I owe you no pot of gold."

"But...but...but..." Mordred sputtered. "The price of the wedding supper alone..."

The princess reached out of the carriage and patted Mordred on the head. "Thanks for everything!" she exclaimed. Then the happy couple galloped off for their honeymoon.

"I'm ruined!" Mordred bellowed. "Ruined!"

He turned to Wiglaf, his violet eyes bulging. "It's all your fault!" he growled.

"*My* fault?" Wiglaf cried.

"If you weren't a redheaded dragon slayer named Wiglaf, none of this would have happened!" Mordred yelled. "I'm going to throw you into the dungeon. It's the Thumb Screws for you, my boy...."

The Sir Lancelot almost-magic ring began flashing a bright orange warning: *Danger, danger, danger!* Wiglaf didn't wait around to hear any more. He took off running. Angus and Erica took off after him. They knew just where to hide from Mordred until his temper cooled down—in the DSA library.

As Wiglaf ran, he felt better than he had felt in a long, long time. He felt as if he really might live happily ever after.

~DSA~
YEARBOOK

Goldius est goodius!

The Campus of Dragon Slayers' Academy

~Our Founders~

Sir Herbert Dungeonstone

Sir Ichabod Popquiz

～ Our Philosophy ～

Sir Herbert and Sir Ichabod founded Dragon Slayers' Academy on a simple principle still held dear today: Any lad—no matter how weak, yellow-bellied, lazy, pigeon-toed, smelly, or unwilling—can be transformed into a fearless dragon slayer who goes for the gold. After four years at DSA, lads will finally be of some worth to their parents, as well as a source of great wealth to this distinguished academy.* ** ***

---

* Please note that Dragon Slayers' Academy is a strictly-for-profit institution.

** Dragon Slayers' Academy reserves the right to keep some of the gold and treasure that any student recovers from a dragon's lair.

*** The exact amount of treasure given to a student's family is determined solely by our esteemed headmaster, Mordred. The amount shall be no less than 1/500th of the treasure and no greater than 1/499th.

Mordred de Marvelous

Mordred graduated from Dragon Bludgeon High, second in his class. The other student, Lionel Flyzwattar, went on to become headmaster of Dragon Stabbers' Prep. Mordred spent years as part-time, semi-substitute student teacher at Dragon Whackers' Alternative School, all the while pursuing his passion for mud wrestling. Inspired by how filthy rich Flyzwattar had become by running a school, Mordred founded Dragon Slayers' Academy in CMLXXIV, and has served as headmaster ever since.

Known to the Boys as: Mordred de Miser
Dream: Piles and piles of dragon gold
Reality: Yet to see a single gold coin
Best-Kept Secret: Mud wrestled under the name Macho-Man Mordie
Plans for the Future: Will retire to the Bahamas . . . as soon as he gets his hands on a hoard

Lady Lobelia

Lobelia de Marvelous is Mordred's sister and a graduate of the exclusive If-You-Can-Read-This-You-Can-Design-Clothes Fashion School. Lobelia has offered fashion advice to the likes of King Felix the Husky and Eric the Terrible Dresser. In CMLXXIX, Lobelia married the oldest living knight, Sir Jeffrey Scabpicker III. That's when she gained the title of Lady Lobelia, but—alas!—only a very small fortune, which she wiped out in a single wild shopping spree. Lady Lobelia has graced Dragon Slayers' Academy with many visits, and can be heard around campus saying, "Just because I live in the Middle Ages doesn't mean I have to look middle-aged."

Known to the Boys as: Lady Lo Lo
Dream: Frightfully fashionable
Reality: Frightful
Best-Kept Secret: Shops at Dark-Age Discount Dress Dungeon
Plans for the Future: New uniforms for the boys with mesh tights and lace tunics

Sir Mort du Mort

Sir Mort is our well-loved professor of Dragon Slaying for Beginners as well as Intermediate and Advanced Dragon Slaying. Sir Mort says that, in his youth, he was known as the Scourge of Dragons. (We're not sure what it means, but it sounds scary.) His last encounter was with the most dangerous dragon of them all: Knightshredder. Early in the battle, Sir Mort took a nasty blow to his helmet and has never been the same since.

Known to the Boys as: The Old Geezer
Dream: Outstanding Dragon Slayer
Reality: Just plain out of it
Best-Kept Secret: He can't remember
Plans for the Future: Taking a little nap

Coach Wendell Plungett

Coach Plungett spent many years questing in the Dark Forest before joining the Athletic Department at DSA. When at last he strode out of the forest, leaving his dragon-slaying days behind him, Coach Plungett was the most muscle-bulging, physically fit, manliest man to be found anywhere north of Nowhere Swamp. "I am what you call a hunk," the coach admits. At DSA, Plungett wears a number of hats—or, helmets. Besides PE Teacher, he is Slaying Coach, Square-Dance Director, Pep-Squad Sponsor, and Privy Inspector. He hopes to meet a damsel—she needn't be in distress—with whom he can share his love of heavy metal music and long dinners by candlelight.

Known to the Boys as: Coach
Dream: Tough as nails
Reality: Sleeps with a stuffed dragon named Foofoo
Best-Kept Secret: Just pull his hair
Plans for the Future: Finding his lost lady love

Brother Dave

Brother Dave is the DSA librarian. He belongs to the Little Brothers of the Peanut Brittle, an order known for doing impossibly good deeds and cooking up endless batches of sweet peanut candy. How exactly did Brother Dave wind up at Dragon Slayers' Academy? After a batch of his extra-crunchy peanut brittle left three children from Toenail toothless, Brother Dave vowed to do a truly impossible good deed. Thus did he offer to be librarian at a school world-famous for considering reading and writing a complete and utter waste of time. Brother Dave hopes to change all that.

Known to the Boys as: Bro Dave
Dream: Boys reading in the libary
Reality: Boys sleeping in the library
Best-Kept Secret: Uses Cliff's Notes
Plans for the Future: Copying out all the lyrics to "Found a Peanut" for the boys

Professor Prissius Pluck

Professor Pluck graduated
from Peter Piper Picked a
Peck of Pickled Peppers Prep,
and went on to become a
professor of Science at
Dragon Slayers' Academy.
His specialty is the Multiple
Choice Pop Test. The boys
who take Dragon Science,
Professor Pluck's popular
class,

a) are amazed at the great
quantities of saliva
Professor P. can project
b) try never to sit in the front row
c) beg Headmaster Mordred to transfer them to
another class
d) all of the above

⚜

Known to the Boys as: Old Spit Face
Dream: Proper pronunciation of *p*'s
Reality: Let us spray
Best-Kept Secret: Has never seen a pippi-hippo-
pappa-peepus up close
Plans for the Future: Is working on a cure for
chapped lips

Staff

Frypot

How Frypot came to be the cook at DSA is something of a mystery. Rumors abound. Some say that when Mordred bought the broken-down castle for his school, Frypot was already in the kitchen and he simply stayed on. Others say that Lady Lobelia hired Frypot because he was so speedy at washing dishes. Still others say Frypot knows many a dark secret that keeps him from losing his job. But no one ever, *ever* says that Frypot was hired because of his excellent cooking skills.

⚜

Known to the Boys as: Who needs a nickname with a real name like Frypot?
Dream: Cleaner kitchen
Reality: Kitchen cleaner
Best-Kept Secret: Takes long bubble baths in the moat
Plans for the Future: Has signed up for a beginning cooking class

Yorick

Yorick is Chief Scout at DSA. His knack for masquerading as almost anything comes from his years with the Merry Minstrels and Dancing Damsels Players, where he won an award for his role as the Glass Slipper in "Cinderella". However, when he was passed over for the part of Mama Bear in "Goldilocks", Yorick decided to seek a new way of life. He snuck off in the night and, by dawn, still dressed in the bear suit, 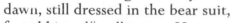 found himself walking up Huntsmans Path. Mordred spied him from a castle window, recognized his talent for disguise, and hired him as Chief Scout on the spot.

Known to the Boys as: Who's that?
Dream: Master of Disguise
Reality: Mordred's Errand Boy
Best-Kept Secret: Likes dressing up as King Ken
Plans for the Future: To lose the bunny suit

Wiglaf of Pinwick

Wiglaf, our newest lad, hails from a hovel outside the village of Pinwick, which makes Toenail look like a thriving metropolis. Being one of thirteen children, Wiglaf had a taste of dorm life before coming to DSA and he fit right in. He started the year off with a bang when he took a stab at Coach Plungett's brown pageboy wig. Way to go, Wiggie! We hope to see more of this lad's wacky humor in the years to come.

Dream: Bold Dragon-Slaying Hero
Reality: Still hangs on to a "security" rag
Extracurricular Activities: Animal-Lovers Club, President; No More Eel for Lunch Club, President; Frypot's Scrub Team, Brush Wielder; Pig Appreciation Club, Founder
Favorite Subject: Library
Oft-Heard Saying: *"Ello-hay, Aisy-day!"*
Plans for the Future: To go for the gold!

Angus du Pangus

The nephew of Mordred and
Lady Lobelia, Angus walks
the line between saying, "I'm
just one of the lads" and
"I'm going to tell my
uncle!" Will this Class I
lad ever become a mighty
dragon slayer? Or will he
take over the kitchen from
Frypot some day? We of
the DSA Yearbook staff are
betting on choice #2. And
hey, Angus? The sooner the
better!

Dream: A wider menu selection at DSA
Reality: Eel, Eel, Eel!
Extracurricular Activities: DSA Cooking Club,
President; Smilin' Hal's Off-Campus Eatery, Sales
Representative
Favorite Subject: Lunch
Oft-Heard Saying: *"I'm still hungry"*
Plans for the Future: To write *101 Ways to Cook a
Dragon*

Eric von Royale

Eric hails from Someplace Far Away (at least that's what he wrote on his Application Form). There's an air of mystery about this Class I lad, who says he is "totally typical and absolutely average." If that is so, how did he come to own the rich tapestry that hangs over his cot? And are his parents really close personal friends of Sir Lancelot? Did Frypot the cook bribe him to start the Clean Plate Club? And doesn't Eric's arm ever get tired from raising his hand in class so often?

Dream: Valiant Dragon Slayer
Reality: Teacher's Pet
Extracurricular Activities: Sir Lancelot Fan Club; Armor Polishing Club; Future Dragon Slayer of the Month Club; DSA Pep Squad, Founder and Cheer Composer
Favorite Subject: All of Them!!!!!
Oft-Heard Saying: *"When I am a mighty Dragon Slayer . . ."*
Plans for the Future: To take over DSA

Baldrick de Bold

This is a banner year for Baldrick. He is celebrating his tenth year as a Class I lad at DSA. Way to go, Baldrick! If any of you new students want to know the ropes, Baldrick is the one to see. He can tell when you should definitely *not* eat the cafeteria's eel, where the choice seats are in Professor Pluck's class, and what to tell the headmaster if you are late to class. Just don't ask him the answer to any test questions.

Dream: To run the world
Reality: A runny nose
Extracurricular Activities: Practice Dragon Maintenance Squad; Least Improved Slayer-in-Training Award
Favorite Subject: *"Could you repeat the question?"*
Oft Heard Saying: *"A dragon ate my homework."*
Plans for the Future: To transfer to Dragon Stabbers' Prep

KNIGHT FOR A DAY

When Wiglaf learns that he has won "A Day
with Sir Lancelot (The World's Most Perfect Knight),"
he can hardly believe it. His friend Erica can't believe it,
either! And when the big day arrives, she is even more
doubtful. Is Erica just jealous, or is there something
fishy about The World's Most Perfect Knight?

About the Author

Kate McMullan taught fourth grade in Los Angeles and sixth grade on an Air Force base in Germany before moving to New York City and becoming an author of over one hundred children's books.

She and her husband, noted illustrator Jim McMullan, collaborated on the I Stink! picture book series, featuring monologues by a garbage truck, a backhoe loader, and other big vehicles. These books are the inspiration behind Amazon's popular animated series for preschoolers *The Stinky & Dirty Show*.

For new readers, Kate created stories about Fluffy, the Classroom Guinea Pig. Her book *Pearl and Wagner: One Funny Day* received a 2010 Geisel Honor.

Dragon Slayers' Academy, Kate's series of early chapter books, features medieval mayhem, bad knock-knock jokes, and a Pig Latin–speaking pig.

For middle graders, Kate has written Myth-O-Mania, the Greek myths as told by Hades.

You can friend Kate on Facebook, follow @katemcmullan1 on Twitter, or visit her website, katemcmullan.com.

Also Available

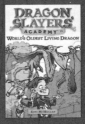